Half-Wild
and
Other Stories
of
Encounter

Half-Wild
and
Other Stories
of
Encounter

I hope you find meaning in these stories.

— Emily Paskevics

EMILY PASKEVICS

Thistledown Press

Thistledown Press Ltd.
Unit 222, 220 20th Street W
Saskatoon SK, S7M 0W9
www.thistledownpress.com

Library and Archives Canada Cataloguing in Publication
Title: Half-wild and other stories of encounter / Emily Paskevics.
Names: Paskevics, Emily, author.
Identifiers: Canadiana 20230191320 | ISBN 9781771872485 (softcover)
Classification: LCC PS8631.A825 H35 2023 | DDC C813/.6—dc23

Cover and book design by Kong Njo
Cover images: © iStock.com
Printed and bound in Canada

Thistledown Press gratefully acknowledges the financial assistance
of The Canada Council for the Arts, SK Arts, and the Government of
Canada for its publishing program.

Canada Council   Conseil des arts
for the Arts   du Canada

sk arts

Canadä

For my sister, Laura

I hope you find meaning in these stories.
— Emily R.

Contents

Bear Bones

It's not yet dawn, and I've woken up all wrong. There's a pressure in my chest and I can't breathe, thinking I've heard her voice—just there, beyond reach, in the dark. *Dad, please come take me home.* Any father can tell you how it is when your kid's in trouble and you're right on the edge. The phone cries out again and I sit up, groping around the nightstand.

My voice is a croak. *Louisa?*

The bed sags under me. It's not my daughter calling, after all—it's the constable from Washago. Haven't heard from him in weeks, and the first thing he tells me is that they still haven't found her. But they've found something.

➤

As a kid, Louisa lived and breathed these woods. Climbing trees, running barefoot in the bush behind our trailer, following the river to the lake, catching pike and gutting them herself, sleeping under the stars, and dreaming of bears. She always had a thing for bears. Perched in a tree, avoiding some kind of trouble she got herself into along the way—and little Louisa was always

1

getting into trouble—she'd look down at me with her big blue eyes and say: *Hey Daddy, did you know in the olden days people thought that if you drank bear's milk, you'd turn into a bear?*

No, I didn't know. I told her to come straight down, but she sassed back: *You'll never catch me!*

Lou grew up but she never stopped getting into trouble. Things got rough when her ma died. It was hard on all of us, watching cancer dwindle a strong woman into dust. At eight years old, Louisa burned up her legs from playing with matches next to the jerry cans of gasoline in the shed. Then her big brother Larry was killed when his Harley collided with a quarry truck at the tricky bend before town I'd always warned him about. He was on his way to pick Lou up from school after she'd been suspended for smoking in the girl's washroom, and she always partway blamed herself. After that it was just the two of us, and we made things work. Hunting and fishing, and the woods, kept us close.

As she got older, Louisa came and went. But she always said these woods were where she felt the safest, the place she most thought of as home. Even when I didn't hear from her for months at a time, I figured that meant something in the end.

> ➤

It's the winter solstice, late afternoon, middle of the worst storm in over a decade. Louisa makes her way through the snowdrifts along Sadowa Road. She's wearing a man's oilskin coat, and it hangs below her knees. Her hair's tucked under the collar, a long, red-brown rope reaching down to her waist.

Sadowa Road means no streetlights all the way to town. It means deer-crossing signs half-battered with buckshot. It means a skinny gravel shoulder veering into the woods, which have been peeled back just enough to reveal a handful of shacks. Louisa approaches the first place she comes across that isn't abandoned: a mobile home with its porch light swinging around in the wind.

The blue-painted door is all scratched up from when a bear tried to get in.

She knocks and steps back, blowing on her hands. An old-timer answers, squinting into the storm, and Louisa asks for a ride to the edge of town. The wife says over his shoulder, *What, hon, in this weather?* But the man says, *All right, I guess,* and starts pulling on his coat. He tells Louisa to wait inside until he gets the truck warmed up. She thanks him, apologizing, but he says it's no problem at all. He heads out, and the wife takes a good, long look at her. Her eyes are kind. She asks, *You in some sort of trouble?* Louisa shakes her head, no.

The wife doesn't believe her but heaves herself up from the narrow couch and rummages around in a cupboard. She hands Lou a twenty-dollar bill and a sandwich bag full of cookies. Louisa protests but the wife insists, pushing the cookies and cash into Louisa's pocket. The man sticks his head in the door, letting in a rush of arctic air, *Okey-dokey, truck's all ready.*

The snow swirls ever thicker as they inch across black ice toward Orillia. The radio's tuned to an AM station—the old pickup doesn't have FM at all, so it's mostly just Elvis crooning through the static. The man smokes, saying it helps him concentrate. He offers Louisa a cigarette too, which she pockets. When they finally reach the edge of town, Louisa says, *You can drop me off here, sir*—meaning the intersection just before Atherley Narrows. There's a deserted gas station at one corner, a pub called Good Folks at another, a strip club adjacent, and nothing else.

The man says, *C'mon, I can't just leave you here.*

Louisa tells him it's fine, but he says he wouldn't be able to sleep knowing he'd left her in the middle of nowhere. He drives on, pointing out a twenty four-hour diner over the bridge. *I'd feel better if you went there,* he says.

She shrugs, rubbing her red-raw hands together. They cross the bridge spanning the Narrows, and as Louisa peers through the snow at Lake Couchiching on her side, the man looks at Lake Simcoe on his.

The pickup stutters to a stop at the turnoff for the diner. The man offers her a hand, but Louisa pushes the door wide to the blustering wind. *You've helped so much already*, she says. Before she closes the door, he calls out, *Hey kid, are you running away, or going someplace?*

Louisa admits that she doesn't know for sure. *But sir, thanks again*. She swings the door shut before he can notice the twenty-dollar bill she's left behind. As she makes her way through the knee-deep snow toward the diner, the pickup crawls back over the bridge and dissolves into the storm.

➤

I roll the window right down as I drive to the police station, preferring the brisk April wind to sucking on my own stale air. There's a tremor in my hands, and my left leg bounces around—it's too much coffee, a lack of sleep, and all these months of waiting and worrying about Lou. When a black bear looms up ahead I slam hard on the brake, lurching forward and nearly cracking my head open on my own knuckles. The truck grazes the guardrail and swerves just short of the ditch before I get control of the wheel again.

For a few seconds, the only sound is the buzzing in my ears. Then, with a gasp, my breathing starts up again like a rusty old machine. The turn signal's clicking. I fiddle it off, and when I look up again, the bear's hardly two metres away from my rolled-down window. She's just standing there scrutinizing the truck. No—she's peering directly at me, her pale gaze fixing on my own.

I tap the horn, hoping to spook her off the road before some-one else comes ripping round the bend. The bear takes a step and hesitates, then rises onto her hind legs, sniffling and huffing. Then, with a grunt, she drops back onto all fours and ambles off the road into the bush, yellow birch and white cedar rearranging themselves behind her.

I drive on toward the police station, my fingers tapping out an agitated refrain on the steering wheel. I turn the radio on, then switch it off again. Thing is, never in my life have I heard of a black bear with blue eyes.

>

As the old man and his truck fade into the snow-blown distance, Lou hitches her collar up to her ears and heads back over the Narrows. It takes half an hour for her to flounder down to the intersection, where the neon sign for Good Folks flashes through the storm. An ambulance struggles by, wailing and swerving down the icy ramp toward the marina. Through the falling snow, she can just make out an upturned pickup on the ice below.

Louisa struggles against the wind till she reaches the parking lot next to the pub, where the county bus stops just before Orillia on its way up past Washago. The last bus left hours ago, and she'll have to wait around till morning. She pulls the oilskin close, bracing herself against the cold. Then the pub's door swings open and two guys stumble out, dragging the last few bars of a Hendrix riff with them. They slouch nearby, their backs to the wind as they fumble in their pockets.

Louisa pulls the cigarette from her own coat pocket and asks, *Got a light?*

Sure do, the leaner guy replies as he pulls out a lighter. He peers at her more closely. *Sure do, baby*, he adds with a wink.

He gives her a familiar onceover as he cups the flame for her. Inhaling, Lou wonders if she knows him, met him on one of those nights she barely remembers at the casino. Exhaling, she doesn't think so. She has a decade on him at least—he hardly looks twenty. They huddle against the brick wall in the howling wind, not talking much. Then the skinny guy asks whereabouts she's from, and where she's headed.

Just north a bit, she says. *Washago.*

That near the casino? he asks.

He edges closer, and Louisa catches the reek of cheap cologne. She holds her breath, keeping the smoke in for a moment longer.

Yeah sure, she shrugs. *Basically.*

The redhead pipes up, *Hey, that's where we're going, eh, Danny?*

We sure are, the skinny one says. *Want a ride?*

Louisa takes one last drag on the cigarette. It's not too far now, home. If something happens, it's two-to-one, sure, but these guys have no real game. She figures that if she can get them to give her a ride partway to Washago, she can walk the rest of the way home.

Yeah, I'll take a ride. Thanks.

Danny smiles wide. *No worries,* he says. *Anything to help out a nice girl like you.*

The wind whips their voices back down their throats. He opens the passenger side of the red sedan and Louisa climbs in, her long braid swinging as she bunches up the heavy folds of her coat around her knees.

Damn, he laughs. *That your daddy's coat or something?*

She doesn't reply, and the door creaks as it shuts her in. It takes Danny three tries to get the car started. He cranks the heat, but it only splutters. Lou directs him north, off the main drag, saying she knows a shortcut to the casino. The road's narrow and full of sharp bends.

After a while, Danny's eyes start flicking from the road to Louisa and back again. She stares straight ahead as he snakes a hand across the seat toward her. The redhead's already passed out and snoring in the back.

God your hair's long, Danny says, stroking her thigh. *Real pretty.*

Louisa sits absolutely still. Snow melts a slow, cold trickle down her spine.

Hey, he tries again. *Buddy's asleep back there. It's just you and me, honey.* Through the bulk of the oilskin, his grip tightens on her leg. *C'mon, baby,* he hisses. *Gimme something.*

He lunges, grabbing Lou by the hair and dragging her head into his lap. The car veers toward the guardrail, jerking them all forward before snapping them back. They hit black ice and Danny jams down hard on the gas instead of the brake. The car slams into the rail with full force—flipping once, then twice, and landing upended by some cedars sagging under the weight of snow.

➤

Two days later, *the Orillia Times* ran a special two-page spread highlighting the deadly aftermath of the storm. Headlines like "Two Teens Killed in Rama Rollover" and "Man in Critical Condition after Pickup Plunges off Bridge" were accompanied by photos of overturned, half-buried vehicles.

Sitting alone at the kitchen table, I cut out a small write-up from the last page of the same paper: "Local Woman Missing." A search party was sent out to scour the woods around Washago for the allotted twenty-four hours, but by then the storm had obliterated any trace of Louisa. In the end, it was mostly just me driving around the dirt roads or snowshoeing through the bush, day after day, looking for a sign.

People had their theories. They said someone must have done her in and it was a tragedy, while others said someone did her in and she had it coming all along. Still others said she got lost, *poor girl, what bad luck.* They all wondered what in hell she was doing out there, anyway—a grown woman should know better than to wander off during a storm. I wondered that myself. But my Louisa knows these woods better than just about anyone else.

≻

Still unsettled from encountering the bear on the road, I lean against the desk at the station as a young cop shows me what they've found. Seems like there's always a different officer on the case, and good luck trying to get any kind of a straight answer. This one's clean shaven and his uniform looks crisp—as though his mother ironed and starched it for him. She probably packed his lunch, too.

He holds out a garbage bag. I look at it, and he looks at me. Then he sets the bag down on the desk, fumbling with the twist-tie, and pulls something out.

At first I think it's some sort of grubby old animal hide, but then I recognize my old oilskin coat. The officer coughs and explains that the coat was found draped over a branch in front of a shallow cave, some fifty kilometres northeast of Atherley Narrows, deep in the bush.

The cave, he says, *was full of bones.* He gestures to a shoebox on the desk.

Then he notices the look on my face. *Bear bones,* he says. *I'm sorry, Mr. Raimondo, I mean it was just bear bones.*

He opens the box. Inside, there's a long-jawed skull the size of a football, a few ribs, a femur, a pelvis, and claws. The bones are already yellowed, at least a few seasons old.

Unrelated, maybe, the officer is saying. *But I dunno, I guess I thought you should know.*

I thank him for his time and drape the coat over my arm. Then I look at the bones and ask if I can take them, too.

≻

In the moments following the crash, the only sound is the buzzing in Louisa's ears. She clears her throat and winces as pain sears up her neck and pounds in her forehead. Her voice is faint when she tries to call out. There's a clicking noise and a vague hissing coming from somewhere under the hood. She can't see the guys, but the only breathing she can hear is her own. Louisa closes her eyes as the storm howls on.

When she comes around again, she's shivering. She struggles with her seatbelt, then crawls out through the busted window on the passenger's side. She stands and braces herself against the wind. Touching her throbbing forehead, her fingers come away streaked with blood. Louisa jams her fists into the deep pockets of her coat, narrowing her eyes into the storm. She takes a few steps away from the car wreck, but the wind's so fierce and the snow's so deep that at first she's not moving in any particular direction.

Gradually, Louisa settles into a heavy, stomping rhythm that leads her away from the wreck and into the spruce woods. Ice encrusts her eyelashes. Arms outstretched, feeling her way through the trees, she lurches on until the dense forest stands between her and the rest of the world.

When she has no strength left, Louisa falls to her knees before a hollowed-out tree. With a final heave, she drags herself into a crevice among the roots, and finds herself in a shallow cave. There's a dog-like smell, but muskier, almost rank. She hunkers down, blowing on her hands before pressing a palm to the wound on her forehead. The blood's congealed into ice. She rearranges her aching limbs under the coat, and as she settles back, Louisa senses a living warmth nearby. She can just make out the shape of a dormant black bear through the shadows.

Louisa makes a sound in the back of her throat, but she isn't afraid. Delirious with cold, she crawls deeper into the cave and curls up against the slumbering form. She takes in its feral scent as the bear snuffles in its torpor, but doesn't stir. Lulled by the steady rumble of its breathing, Louisa's own breath slows as she grows drowsy and warm. One by one, she nibbles at the cookies from the sandwich bag in her pocket. Soon, she slips into the slow, rhythmic lull of bear time, drifting through what remains of the long, cold season.

It will be the spring equinox before Louisa lumbers out of the den like some creature the land itself dreamed up. She'll be ravenous and itchy, with a dense fur coat of her own. All she'll remember of the winter is that she was lost, and she found her way home.

Bird Sanctuary

The slingshot belonged to my father. He used it to whip pebbles at our dog when he wouldn't shut up, and once he took out the eyeball of a fox that got too close to the chickens we used to keep behind the trailer. Dad taught me to aim at stacked beer cans, and I made him proud with my hawk-eyed precision. I could knock off each can on my first try. *My little Annie Oakley*, he called me. Those were the good times, back before the fighting.

Picking through a box of Dad's stuff that Mom was getting ready to take to the dump, I'd found the old slingshot and claimed it as a kind of trophy. The rubber band was a little loose but still stretchy, and the polished wood was slightly sticky. I also saved a red flannel jacket of his. It was far too big for me, with deep front pockets, but I wore it nearly every day despite Mom's insistence that it was unflattering. I knew it annoyed her, seeing me with Dad's stuff. She was also pissed because I'd flunked a grade and was already skipping my way through most of the second round. She said I was turning out just like him. I slammed the door as I went out.

I wandered around for a while, trudging along an unpaved backroad and pocketing a few good-sized stones along the way. I could've gone to the water tower, the train tracks, the cemetery—all the places I usually went when I skipped class or needed to get away from Mom. But just about everyone went to those spots, hanging out, eating pizza, making out, blasting music from their beat-up old trucks. So I headed for the one place I figured no one I knew would ever go.

The bird sanctuary, along the northern shore of Wagner's Lake, was marshy and overgrown with willow, mostly left to its own devices by visitors and conservation authorities alike. Aside from the occasional four-wheeler roaming the edges of the wetland, the area was truly the wild domain of the birds it was intended to protect. The marsh was a piece of Crown land that wasn't even listed on the map—Google only indicated an unlabeled patch of green that a skinny, unnamed creek drained through on its way to somewhere else.

I picked my way along a mossy boardwalk that carved a path along the creek, leading deeper into the marsh. The surrounding reeds were taller than I was, forming a green, whispering wall between me and the rest of the world. I hopped from one busted plank to the next. I was so focused on not losing my footing that a sudden, violent rustling and braying just behind me nearly sent me belly-flopping into the water. Heart thrashing, I covered my head with my arms as the air filled with loud honking and flapping. A goose landed on the boardwalk ahead of me, lifting its wings and craning its neck in my direction.

I reached into the pocket of my flannel jacket for a stone and the slingshot. As I aimed, the goose spread its wings and took off—I let the stone fly and he came tumbling down, hitting the water with a smack.

The slingshot dangled from my fingers as I stared at the bent reeds where the goose had fallen. Then I heard more trampling and splashing coming in my direction. I couldn't see a thing through the reeds, and I dropped to a crouch as I looked wildly around. A startled bear, I thought, or worse—a rampaging moose. I braced myself, the slingshot suddenly feeling limp and useless in my fist.

But it was just a guy from school, John Monkman. He was charging through the marsh toward me, boots sucking mud, a half-crazed look in his pale grey eyes. Binoculars were swinging from a cord around his neck. He stopped short, looking just as surprised as I was—even appalled—to find me crouching there on the boardwalk. I stood up, tucking the slingshot into my jacket pocket.

"Hey," I said.

He was panting and up to his knees in dark-brown water. John Monkman and I were the only two kids bussed to the local high school from the nearby trailer park that was half-drowning in the marsh. He was held back a year in middle school before they realized he wasn't actually slow, just a weirdo who mostly kept to himself. At school, people called him the Monk.

The only other thing I knew about him was that his brother was killed in a car crash a while back, and John Monkman had been the driver.

"Did you see him?" he demanded.

I shrugged. I didn't know who he was talking about. I watched as he poked around until he spotted the goose sprawled among the reeds—misshapen, wings all wrong. He gasped as he took in the damage.

"Shit," he said, as he waded in slow motion through the water. "I'm so sorry, buddy."

Still murmuring apologies, the Monk carried the goose over to the boardwalk a few feet from where I was standing. He set it down gently, tucked in its wings, and straightened its neck. A vaguely fishy smell mingled with the reek of leaf rot around us.

"Friend of yours?" I asked.

He glanced up at me but didn't reply. He prodded at the goose's chest with his fingertips.

"Heartbeat," he said, more to himself than to me. "He's just stunned."

He stepped back just as the goose kicked, flapped its powerful wings, and careened into flight. We could still hear the bird honking long after it had disappeared across the lake. The Monk pumped his fist in the air. I took a deep breath, and when he turned to face me I grinned. He didn't smile back.

"What was that about?" I asked.

He turned away and climbed out of the water onto the boardwalk. He fiddled with one of the straps on his chest waders, which were faded and oversized, as though they belonged to somebody else.

"I heard his distress call," he said at last. "So I came as quickly as I could."

"And you just happen to be all geared up and dressed like a duck?" I laughed.

He scowled. "What are you doing here, anyway?"

"It's a bird sanctuary, isn't it? So maybe I came here to pray."

I snorted at my own joke, but the Monk's eyebrows didn't unfurrow. Suddenly I felt like the one who didn't belong there, an intruder. He made his way past me and I followed him down the boardwalk, hopping awkwardly over the busted planks.

"I hope he'll be okay," I offered. "The goose."

"Dunno." He raised his binoculars, scanning the sky. "Not sure what happened. The goslings just hatched, so I was worried when I saw—if one of the parents gets killed, their chances of survival are—you know, even less. But that one's a yearling, so he hasn't mated yet. He's not part of a crèche, either."

"Oh," I said. After a pause, I asked, "What's a crèche?"

"It's when a few adult geese within a flock group together to help raise the young," he said, still peering through the binoculars.

A little bird was perched on the tip of a nearby reed. "Increases their chances of survival."

"That's pretty smart of them," I said, impressed.

He looked at me, and I was surprised to read a hint of satisfaction in his expression.

"There's a flock that returns every year," he said, lowering the binoculars again when the little bird darted away. "I've been watching them for so long that I know most of them by their individual voices. You get kind of attached. There are so many other birds—kingfishers, loons, great blue herons, ospreys—but I like the geese. They're so familiar, so common, and because of that, most people don't like them."

"Right," I said, thinking I'd never heard John Monkman say so much at once.

"Did you know that Canada geese can live up to twenty years?"

Unless they're brought down by some idiot with a slingshot, I thought with a creeping sense of shame. As we walked through the marsh, the Monk proceeded to tell me a bunch of facts about geese, including how adaptable they are, how they tend to mate for life, how far they fly when they go south. He knew a lot, and it was actually pretty interesting. I'd always thought of the geese as a noisy honking nuisance, leaving their green shit everywhere for the dog to eat and puke back up.

I watched the Monk from the corner of my eye as he raised his binoculars again. He wasn't bad-looking, really, despite the waders. His sandy hair was slightly matted, but he was tanned from spending so much time outdoors. I started wondering what it would be like to kiss him, but he kept going on about birds. He pointed out a red-winged blackbird and a wood thrush, and imitated their calls.

At the end of the boardwalk, we headed off in opposite directions without saying goodbye. I took the long way around the lake to get home, following the muddy shoreline and wondering what John Monkman might know about me. Eva Armand, the girl who was always late and cut class to smoke up; the girl who had a different boyfriend every month. The girl whose father had a thing for women half his age.

>

I visited the bird sanctuary several times the following week, watching the geese and feeling pleased with myself when I could remember the names of other birds I saw among the willows and out on the water—common merganser, mallard duck, cedar waxwing. Sometimes I joined the Monk as he plodded through the weeds in his bulky waders. I always had a feeling that he was around, even if I couldn't see him as I made my way through the reeds alone. I wondered if he ever spied on me with those binoculars that were always dangling around his neck.

On one of those solitary afternoons I sat down on the boardwalk and lit a cigarette. I watched a red-winged blackbird bobbing up and down on a reed as he trilled out his throaty song. I'd grown fond of the species, even though the Monk had told me that they were aggressive little patriarchs with a harem of several mates each. From what he'd told me, birds in general were a pretty promiscuous bunch.

Then, in a single strike, a huge brown bird swooped down and snapped up the red-winged blackbird in its talons. I cried out and dropped the cigarette into the water. The large bird landed on a nearby branch and I watched with dismay and fascination as it devoured the smaller bird in a flurry of feathers and viscera.

After the bird flew off, I jumped up and roamed along the boardwalk, looking for the Monk. I whistled a few times, and soon enough he emerged from the bulrushes clutching his binoculars. I told him about the encounter, exaggerating a little when it came to the guts. He extracted a small field guide from the front pocket of his waders and, still standing in the shallows, shuffled the pages until he landed on a series of images of hawks and other birds of prey. I described what I'd seen—the striped chest, the wide wingspan, the fan-shaped tail—and we concluded that it must have been a broad-winged hawk. The Monk told me that they migrated all the way to and from Central America, or sometimes even the Amazon, every year.

He seemed so impressed by the grisly scene I'd witnessed that I half expected him to kiss me. Instead, we sat under a willow tree and took turns scanning the sky with his binoculars, searching for the steady, circular flight patterns of hawks and eagles all afternoon. We were sitting so close together that I could feel the warmth of his body. I breathed in the pine-smoke scent of him.

But the Monk never made a pass at me. I wondered if he might be shy, or maybe some kind of religious. Gradually, I realized that he just wasn't interested. Our excursions into the marsh together weren't a way to try and get into my pants. He genuinely loved being there, surrounded by the reeds and crooked little trees whose roots were steeping in muddy water, and above all he loved the birds. His full attention was always on them, and sometimes it seemed as though it made no difference to him if I was there at all.

I started looking forward to spending time at the sanctuary, whether observing baby birds learning to fly, closing my eyes and listening for particular bird calls, or even witnessing that hawk capturing its prey. I bought a pair of binoculars from the rummage sale at the People's Church in town. One of the lenses was busted, but if I closed my left eye slightly I could still get a decent view. We watched the birds and consulted his worn out field guide, and I no longer thought about come-ons or make-out sessions. I even watched the splashy mating ritual of a pair of loons without casting him a sidelong glance.

But I still hadn't fessed up about the goose I'd shot down on that first day. I figured there was no need to tell him. It was a secret I'd swallowed down, even as I still carried the slingshot deep in the pocket of my flannel jacket, next to the binoculars. I'd never asked him about the car crash or his brother, and the Monk himself never talked about anything but the birds—as though the world beyond the marsh simply didn't exist while we were there, surrounded by reeds and stagnant water.

A couple of times I offered to drive him home in Mom's pickup, since we both lived over on the other side of the lake. But even when we were caught in a lightning storm that just about split the sky open, the Monk refused to accept a ride. When I followed him through the slashing rain along the dirt road, hollering at him to just get in already or he'd drown, he waved me off so aggressively that I finally stopped offering rides.

➤

We found the injured goose floundering alone in shallow water, emitting a series of soft, staccato distress calls. I stood back as the Monk approached the bird, murmuring and making little cluck-ing sounds in the back of his throat. The goose snapped a wing at him in warning. But then, as though the effort was too much, its entire body went limp.

"It's that same goose," he said, and I knew he meant the one I'd shot down on that first day at the sanctuary. "It's definitely him."

"How do you know?"

"His tail feathers," he said. "See the random white one, there? Makes him stand out. I call him Icarus."

He flushed, and that's when I learned that sometimes he named his favourites among the wild birds we observed.

"I don't see any sign that he was attacked, or any damage to his wings or anything. Maybe it's internal." He paused. "We could take him to the wildlife centre in town."

With a bad taste in my mouth, I watched him pull a pair of rubber gloves from the side pockets of his waders. As he gathered up the goose, Icarus stayed limp in the Monk's arms, as though he'd passed out, but one of his black eyes fixed beadily on me as I lagged behind. We headed up to the dirt road, where I'd parked Mom's truck. The dog's crate was in the back, and as I fiddled with the rusty latch it was the Monk's turn to hang back.

"Maybe I'll just walk." He kicked at a stone on the side of the road.

"You can't be serious," I said. "It's at least an *hour* to town on foot. And what am I going to do if the fucking bird—if Icarus—wakes up and starts honking and shitting all over the place? No way."

"I can't," he said, his voice cracking.

"You have to," I said, gesturing at the open cage. "Unless you want to just wait around and watch him die."

He stood there struggling, the goose still cradled in his arms. Then he came round the truck and placed Icarus inside the cage, carefully rearranging his wings and neck. I opened the passenger's side and the Monk climbed in. He sat there rigidly, as though the seat was jabbing his butt with nails. I revved the engine and did a U-turn off the gravel shoulder, showing off a little. I eased off the gas when I saw that his face was deathly pale.

"You really don't like driving, eh?" I said, guiding the truck around the next bend as smoothly as I could. "Because of your brother?"

He shifted in the seat, and all I could see was the back of his sunburned neck. After a strained moment, he nodded.

"That's rough," I said.

We drove in silence until I could no longer stand it.

"My dad taught me to drive," I said. "I was just ten, maybe eleven the first time. I was terrified, obviously, and could barely even reach the pedals. But the more I cried, the more he insisted that I get in and drive. And so I did, seeing as I didn't have a choice with him standing there and yelling at me. But then I always had a blast, rip-roaring on all these back roads with him."

I slowed as we hit a washboardy section of the road.

"I heard he left," the Monk said.

It was strange, finally hearing the words said out loud. In the weeks and months since Dad had taken off, Mom and I hadn't actually spoken about it. We'd just continued doing normal things—me sleeping through my alarm every morning, Mom making TV dinners and telling me off for skipping class, me sassing back. We took turns filling in the gaps where Dad had been—I picked up the mail and Mom dealt with the creditors.

"Yeah," I said. "Yeah, he's gone."

I sensed his eyes on me but kept my gaze fixed on the road. I didn't have much to say after that. The Monk kept his hands tightly clenched in his lap as we drove on, and the only other thing he said was a half-panicked *slow down* as I picked up speed along the rutted road into town. When we pulled up in front of the wildlife centre, he leapt from the truck as though it were on fire. Behind the bars of the cage, Icarus was glassy eyed. I swallowed down the sour taste at the back of my throat.

The Monk disappeared inside the centre with the goose. I settled on the tailgate of the truck, swinging my legs and smoking as I waited. An unseen bird called from a nearby bush, and I tried to determine whether it was a robin or some kind of sparrow. Just as I guessed it could be a robin, some other kind of thrush I'd never seen before flitted out from among the leaves. Just when you think you know a bird, they trick you into thinking they're somebody else.

When the Monk re-emerged twenty minutes later, he was carrying a sealed garbage bag in his arms. I hopped off the truck, not looking at him as I banged the tailgate shut.

"So he didn't make it," I said.

The Monk set the bag in the back and, after the slightest hesitation, climbed into the truck himself.

"It was too late," he said, slumping back against the seat. "I convinced them to let me take him back—for natural decomposition, I guess. I'll bury him at the marsh."

"Okay," I said, as the truck shuddered to life.

"They found a stone lodged in his abdomen," he said, when we were already halfway to the marsh. "There was internal damage."

I rolled the window down to let in some fresh air, my stomach roiling, and after a few minutes the Monk did the same on his side. We didn't speak much for the rest of the drive. I'd hardly brought the truck to a juddering stop at the marsh before he jumped out and slammed the door.

"I can take care of this myself," he called as he retrieved the garbage bag from the back.

I twisted the key in the ignition, and the engine caught. I hadn't meant to kill the bird and I didn't want to have to look at its dead body, thinking the entire time of how I'd messed everything up. But I sat back, watching the Monk making his way down to the weedy shoreline with the garbage bag in his arms. Even if he didn't know it was my fault, I had a feeling that the marsh did, somehow.

I switched the truck off, swearing as I got out, and followed him into the marsh. Maybe it was because I'd glimpsed how he lived with the terrible thing he never mentioned but was surely always on his mind—the accident, his brother's death, his own hands on the wheel. Maybe it was because of how lovingly he handled the goose, or just because I always seem to throw a wrench into things. But as I trailed him through the reeds, I finally told the Monk the truth.

"Look," I said, struggling through the mud. "You remember that day—the first day I was here, when the goose—when Icarus—fell from the sky?"

"Yeah?" He said, setting the goose down in order to scan the far shore with his binoculars.

"Yeah, it was because of me. I shot him."

The back of my throat burned as I confessed. The Monk lowered the lenses slowly, almost reluctantly, and blinked at me.

"Shot him?" He said the words as though they were in a language he didn't quite understand.

I took the slingshot from my pocket and dangled it before him. He looked at the slingshot, then right at me. I stared him down. His expression hardened as his gaze met mine—as though he was really looking this time.

He came at me suddenly, and my mouth filled with the tin-taste of blood as my jaw jammed into his chest. I spat as we grappled, losing our footing in the slippery muck. I held him close and a crow levelled a single hoarse note at us as we tumbled, still struggling, into the shallows.

I shoved him off. He sat up and wiped mud from his eyes with the back of his hand. When he stood, one of his knees cracked. He hoisted the garbage bag over his shoulder.

"I shouldn't have—" he began, but I waved his words away.

"Look, I'm really sorry," I said as I struggled to my feet. "I fucked up. It was before I knew about the birds. Before you told me their names."

I wiped my face clean with a sleeve of my flannel shirt. "I'll help you bury him, if you want."

The only sound around us was the wind shifting through the reeds. Then a wood thrush warbled a series of fluid, flute-like notes from a willow nearby. The Monk met my gaze. He nodded, and I rolled up my sleeves. We began breaking up the earth among the roots of the willow with our bare hands. The dirt was soft, with a rich vegetable smell that didn't quite cover up the distinct undertones of leaf rot.

When we'd dug deep enough, the Monk picked up Icarus as though the goose were a baby and set him in the hole, tucking in the wings and neck. He paused, clearing his throat, and I thought he was about to give a eulogy or something. But all he said was,

Good luck, little buddy. I mumbled, *Sorry.* Nearby, a woodpecker drummed away at a hollow trunk.

As we scooped dirt over the feathers, I thought of the slingshot in my pocket. When I pulled it out, the Monk shot me a look and I put my hands up in a gesture of surrender. Then I snapped the slingshot in half before placing it in the hole. We finished the burial by pressing the earth with our palms, so that when we stepped away the disturbance was barely noticeable among the roots.

We spent the rest of the afternoon sitting on the boardwalk with our bare feet dangling in the water, imitating birdcalls across the lake: crow, loon, cardinal, goose. We laughed at our lame attempts, although he was far more skilled at it than I was. Later on, we parted at the end of the boardwalk and headed our separate ways.

Daughters

Anya leaned toward the smoke and scraped the remaining bulrush roots and wild garlic from the skillet onto her plate. After dragging the battered red canoe ashore for the evening—muscles aching after half a day's worth of paddling upstream—she had gathered the roots and greens, and mixed them with beans, crackers, and the salt-and-pepper mix from her pack.

"Not so bad, is it, girls?" she said.

Christie didn't look up. At thirteen, she was determined to hate everything about the four-day canoe trip into the back-country. Mel, nine-almost-ten, glanced sidelong at her scowling sister before nodding at her mother.

"Better than I thought," she said with her mouth full.

Mel had helped her mother gather the roots after they set up camp, eyeing the muddy bulbs Anya passed her as they both stood ankle-deep at the marshy shoreline. Then Anya demonstrated how to scrape off the root hairs and peel away the outer rind before placing them in the fire for roasting. By that point, the sun was already setting. As they waited for the food to heat up, Anya had imitated the rippling calls of a pair of loons from across the lake. She showed her daughters how to cup their hands as they in turn tried to echo the reedy notes, just has Anya's own mother had showed her. The loons had fallen silent.

"This is gross." Christie spat some half-chewed bulrush root into the fire, where it sizzled and smoked.

"Don't eat it, then." Anya kept her voice level. "Have some of the freeze-dried lasagna instead."

Christie made a face. She hadn't stopped complaining since before they had piled into the car for the two-hour drive north. There was an unfortunate incident early on, barely an hour into the drive to the park, when the car's check engine light flickered on and they stopped at the next gas station. The attendant, a young guy who was probably in his late teens, had offered to take a look at the engine—to Anya's relief and Christie's red-faced dismay. Anya had chatted with him amiably as he checked under the hood while Christie writhed with embarrassment in the backseat.

But Anya had also noticed the sidelong glance he had cast at her eldest daughter as Christie slipped out of the car to buy a coke at the vending machine, her curly auburn hair coming loose from its ponytail. Christie had gotten her first period the previous month, and Anya suddenly felt as though she was running out of time—there was so much she wanted to show the girls, stories she wanted to tell them, before it was too late and they slipped away from her.

Mel had wandered into a nearby abandoned lot and was assessing wildflowers in her well-worn volume of the *Ontario Nature Guide*. Anya knew she still had a bit of time with Mel, who was bookish and serious and sometimes seemed young for her age.

Back on the road, Christie had given both her mother and sister the silent treatment until their next pit stop at a rundown Tim Hortons in the middle of nowhere. Only then, between bites of a maple-dipped donut, did she comment that if their father were there, he wouldn't have needed to ask for help because he would've been able to fix it himself.

"Shut *up*, Christie," her sister said.

"It's all just part of the adventure," Anya said lightly.

Christie shook her head in disgust. Anya took a sip of her coffee and flinched as it seared her tongue and sloshed down her shirt.

"Oh, for *fuck's* sake," she finally snapped. "Christie, stop acting like the world's out to get you. Mel, don't talk like that to your sister. No swearing."

There was a pause before Mel muttered over her Boston cream donut: "*You* just swore, Mom."

Anya had wiped at the stain spreading down her front. Mel was trying to suck the cream from the donut through a little hole she had dug with her pinky finger. But Anya could tell that Christie, still sulking, saw the minor issue with the car as more evidence of her mother's unforgivable flaws.

The separation had happened three years ago, but Dan had recently announced his plans to move down south to the city, motivating them to finalize the divorce earlier that year. In the critical eye of her eldest daughter, Anya knew she was somehow to blame for the final split. Christie had picked up on some of her father's critiques: Anya spent more time in her own imaginary world than in the real world with the rest of them; she wandered off into the woods for hours at a time, even at night; she had a habit of looking through people rather than at them.

Anya stood and placed another log on the fire, then stepped back from the shower of sparks.

"It's a good fire, Mel." She settled into a cross-legged position near the flames. "Great job."

Mel beamed.

The three of them listened to the lake lapping at the shore in little waves. Then something wailed in the distance.

"Was that a wolf?" Mel whispered, eyes wide.

"Don't be stupid," Christie snapped. "Obviously it's a train."

The wail came again, but this time the sound broke into pieces as it faded—a howl dwindling into a distinct series of barks. Christie tried to appear nonchalant and Mel shuffled closer to Anya. An inward calm came over Anya as she put an arm around the little girl and gazed into the darkness beyond the fire. This was her world, in between tame and wild. This was the world she knew best.

"I don't think it's a train, Christie," she said, fanning away smoke. "But it isn't a wolf, either."

She was interrupted by more yips, closer this time. Christie got to her feet, alarmed.

"How do you know they aren't wolves?" she demanded. "Listen, that's *howling*. It's definitely howling!"

Mel looked up at her mother. "You ever heard a wolf howl in real life, Mom?"

Anya threw her head back and did her best impression of the packs she had grown up alongside in the far north. *Ah-ah-wooooo!* She drew it into a long, lonely note that only tapered out when she ran out of breath. Both girls were staring at her.

"Oh my god, Mom." Christie drew back. "You're embarrassing yourself."

"They're coyotes," Anya said. "They won't bother us." She gave Mel a squeeze. "You can check your field guide tomorrow."

They settled into silence again, broken only by the occasional far-off yip or snap from the fire. Then Mel sat up, cleared her throat, and let out a howl of her own—a shrill, wavering screech that sounded more like a cat getting its tail stomped on.

Anya clapped, laughing. "That's pretty good! You're a natural. Bet your sister couldn't top that."

"Yeah, your turn, Christie," Mel said. "Howl!"

Christie scowled at her mother and sister from across the fire, her face flushed from the flames.

"You can't be serious," she said.

"Oh, come on! There's no one around. Howl, Christie."

"I dare you!" Mel added.

"This is so stupid." Christie tossed her Styrofoam plate of cold beans and roots into the flames. "I'm done."

She unzipped the tent's fly, kicking off her sandals and zipping herself inside.

Anya and Mel lay back. They gazed up at the dizzying thickness of stars until Mel started nodding off and the fire was reduced to glowing embers. Then they crawled into the tent and settled into sleeping bags on either side of Christie's unmoving form. Mel fell asleep straightaway, and for a long time Anya listened to her daughters' rhythmic breathing in the snug enclosure of the tent. She'd always wanted to bring the girls to the wilderness park, where her own mother had worked as a backcountry warden at a time when there were few women in the profession. It was from her mother that Anya had learned wildcrafting, animal tracking, and outdoor survival skills. Now she wanted to show her own daughters.

She crept back outside, spread her sleeping bag on the ground near the smoking remains of the fire, and drifted—half dreaming, half keeping watch—until morning.

➤

The trio woke just before dawn, packed up camp, and got an early start on the day. They paddled along the lake's muddy shoreline until they reached a deep and slow-moving river just before noon. The river would lead them to a special spot upstream, a secret waterfall deep in the bush, miles from any trail, that Anya's mother had come across decades ago.

Anya assured her daughters that they were almost there, but as they rounded bend after bend of the river with no sign of the waterfall, she started to doubt herself. Had they been following the wrong tributary for the past day and a half? Maybe she was too confident in assuming that she didn't need a map.

Christie was jabbing at the water with her paddle, slowing them down rather than propelling them forward. Mel whined about her arms hurting. Both were turning pink from sun exposure as they batted away mosquitoes with rising frustration. Soon the girls had joined forces in complaining about aches, bugs, and boredom. Anya gritted her teeth as she pointed to the painted turtles sunning themselves on mossy, half-submerged logs—but by that point, even Mel seemed indifferent to their surroundings.

At last, the river widened into a dark pool surrounded by towering aspen and spruce, with a narrow waterfall cascading down from a tall shelf of white rock at the far end. White lilies drifted on the surface of the water, and purple and yellow wildflowers nodded along the shoreline. It looked like a fragment of tropical paradise somehow transplanted into the northern Ontario wilderness.

"Wow!" Mel said, pointing up. "Look!"

A red-tailed hawk swooped overhead, emitting a plaintive cry, and even Christie seemed in awe of the scenic view before them. Anya gazed around as the canoe drifted through the eddying pool, the paddle in her hands still poised for another stroke.

"Yes, this must be it," she said. "But it looks different. I remember it being bigger, somehow."

"This is actually pretty nice," Christie said.

Anya kept her confusion to herself as they disembarked and dragged the canoe onto the rocky bank. She remembered the falls being a looming presence surrounded by immense conifers, water thundering over white rock into the crystal pool below.

As they located a spot clear of roots and rocks to pitch their tent on, Christie pointed to a pile of what looked like sunbaked nuggets and wrinkled her nose.

"Is that some kind of animal crap?"

Anya crouched to inspect it, rubbing a few nuggets between her thumb and first two fingers. It crumbled to dust in her hands.

"Gross, Mom!" Christie exclaimed.

"It's moose scat," Anya said, brushing her hands off on her jeans as she stood and scanned the surrounding area. "But it's quite old. Now *that*—" she nodded toward a faint imprint in the dried black earth nearby, "that's a predator's paw print." She smiled happily at her girls' tired faces.

Anya's mother had taught her that animal tracking was a way to pay closer attention to the forest's own stories. She remembered her mother squatting, showing her how to read her surroundings, rendering the forest legible through the myriad paths of the creatures that called it home.

"What kind of predator?" Mel crouched next to her mother.

"Well, let's see." Anya placed her hand next to the track. "It's pretty big, isn't it? Notice the shape. Canine tracks usually have definite claw marks and have a kind of oval shape—longer than they are wide. Feline tracks—mountain lions, for instance —rarely show claw marks, and they have a more circular shape— usually wider than they are tall."

"So which one is it?" Mel asked.

"It's hard to tell." Anya sat back on her haunches. "The impression is too faint. It can take years to really learn how to track—it's like learning to read all over again, only you are reading stories the land made up. Your grandma taught me that."

She could see Mel's bewilderment at the lack of a clear answer.

"It can't be a mountain lion," Christie scoffed. "Who's ever heard of mountain lions around here? What a joke."

Anya gave her a long look. Mountain lions, or cougars, had certainly called that particular region of Northwestern Ontario home—if not now, then in the recent past. Anya knew this because she'd had the rare experience of encountering one herself. Her breath caught in her throat as she realized that it was time to tell her daughters her story. She had been saving it for them, waiting for the right age, the right moment, to tell them both together.

"You're right, in one sense." She settled cross-legged next to the track. "They're considered extinct in this region, or at least severely endangered. Which means, of course, that they belong here."

"I don't believe that," Christie said.

"I'm going to tell you a story," Anya said, ignoring her, "about the time I met a mountain lion. Right here, in these very woods."

She motioned for the girls to join her. Mel, still clutching her field guide, sat next to her, with the paw print between them. Christie leaned back against a nearby boulder, arms folded across her chest.

It was a few months after Mel's birth, Anya began. Christie was a toddler. Anya's mother had recently passed away, and Anya had come to the wilderness park to scatter her ashes among the trees. She'd only planned to go for a solo hike for a few hours, but somehow got lost along the way. As dusk settled through the woods, with a full moon rising, she was still wandering along an unfamiliar section of the trail.

"There's nothing like being alone in the forest at night." She lowered her voice so the girls had to move closer to hear her over the dull roar of the waterfall behind them. "And then I heard a growl."

She explained how she'd only had a tiny keychain flashlight, and in its feeble glow she saw a pair of eyes gleaming at her through the darkness. Then the moonlight flashed on the muscular flank of a large animal moving toward her. It was a mountain lion, lean and agile. Anya had grabbed a femur-thick felled branch that she managed to hoist over her left shoulder like an oversized baseball bat, and struck a defensive stance as she tried to talk the wildcat down in a calm voice—all the while bracing for the inevitable attack.

Anya had her daughters' full attention. Both girls were staring at her, wide-eyed.

When the mountain lion lunged, pushing off his powerful haunches and hurtling through the air toward her throat, Anya registered glistening fangs and hot, stinking breath as she swung with all the force she could summon, the branch thudding into the animal's jaw and throwing his head hard to one side, spraying Anya's face with saliva and blood as he fell to the ground.

Anya dropped to her knees from the force of the impact. The branch had shattered in her hands, leaving her with a spear-like fragment.

The mountain lion shook himself off and turned to face her again. This time, she didn't wait for him to attack—she lunged with the sharp stick before her like a sword and he snarled and screamed as the stick jammed into an eyeball. He clawed at her leg as she twisted away and ran blindly through the woods.

"I ran and ran." Anya's voice was hoarse. "On and on through the bush, not knowing where I was going—not knowing any-thing—just that running was my only hope for survival. Then, all of a sudden, I lost my footing and I was falling—sliding, really—down a rocky slope. I landed hard, and I must've struck my head. That's all I remember of that night."

Mel drew in a sharp breath, and looked at her sister. Christie was stony faced. Anya took a deep breath and recounted that when she finally came to, the sun was already rising. Her body ached all over, and she'd lost a lot of blood from the wound in her leg. She became aware of a distant roaring sound, and realized that she was at the waterfall—almost exactly where the three of them were sitting now. She was found a few hours later by some day hikers, who alerted the new park warden.

Anya tugged the left leg of her cargo shorts up to her thigh, exposing three deep scratch marks, three or four inches in length, the colour of mulberry stains. The girls had seen these marks before, but she'd always said they were from a fall when she was younger. Which was sort of true.

"I can still feel them." She ran a finger along the raised scars. "The claws, digging in."

Anya had often imagined telling this story to her daughters over the years, wanting to have them alone with her, in this exact spot by the falls. She'd imagined them exclaiming: *Really, Mom? You fought off a mountain lion?* But the girls were quiet. Mel started picking at a scab on her knee. It was Christie who spoke first.

"That's not what Dad says, you know."

Anya stiffened at the revelation that Dan had already told them—that they had heard his version first. She'd only told him the full story once, while she was still in the hospital in the aftermath of the encounter, her leg and head bandaged and aching.

"Be careful, Anya." He'd enunciated each word deliberately, as though he were carefully arranging a handful of beads on a string. "Some people might call you crazy for telling a story like that."

"But it's true," she'd said, taken aback. She had the stitches to prove it.

He said something about the grieving process, about post-partum depression. He added that it was probably better if she didn't go around telling people about it—especially the girls, even as they got older.

"You'll put nonsense in their heads," he said. "Making them think there are predators all over the place."

But there are predators all over the place, she'd thought. They didn't speak of it again.

Anya met Christie's defiant gaze. She cleared her throat as she straightened her shorts back over the scars.

"Oh really?" Her voice sounded thin. "What does your father say, then?"

"He says you had depression after Mel was born, or whatever. Then Grandma died and you ran off and disappeared for a couple of days. He said you came back covered in scratches and bruises, your clothes all torn up like you'd been running around in the bush like a crazy person."

"Your father wasn't there," Anya said.

"He said you had to be hospitalized."

"Yes," Anya faltered. "For the injuries—my leg, the concussion—"

She wanted to backtrack—to tell the story again, but slower, with more detail, so that her daughters would really hear her and understand what she meant. She didn't quite know why she had to tell them this story, or what they would do with it, but she needed them to know what she had survived.

Christie was gazing in the direction of the waterfall. Mel flipped noisily through the pages of her field guide.

"They don't have mountain lions in here," she announced. "But maybe it was a bobcat?" she flipped another page. "Or a lynx."

"Check for *cougar*," Anya said. "That's another name for it."

"Just bobcat and lynx," Mel said, after a pause. "Those are the only two wildcats in the book."

Christie scoffed, and Anya resisted the urge to tear the guide from her daughter's hand and chuck it into the fire.

"Well," she said. "You have to remember that a forest is alive. It changes, adapts over time. Animals leave, and sometimes they come back. The book can only tell you about what you might expect to see. But being here and experiencing the forest for itself, you might be surprised."

Mel looked down at the field guide in her lap, then up at her mother.

"Oh." She finally set the book aside. After a long pause punctuated by the chittering cries of nearby kingfishers, Mel asked: "Can we go swimming?"

Anya opened her mouth, then closed it again. She nodded as she stood, rubbing at her tense lower back. "Of course. Let's go swimming."

"Not me," Christie said, turning away and walking purposefully toward the faint trail that led up the side of the ridge. "I'm going for a walk."

"Don't go too far," Anya called after her.

Only the stiffening of her stride indicated that Christie had heard her mother. She didn't glance back. Anya held a towel up for Mel to change into her swimsuit, watching as Christie disappeared among the trees. She took a deep breath, held it in, then let it go with a sigh.

"Will you come in with me?" Mel asked, as Anya helped re-adjust the shoulder straps of her swimsuit. The faded pink fabric gave off a faint chlorine smell.

Anya looked out at the swirling pool and the relentless, white-crested cascade. Her memory of the spot was already fading, redrawn by its living presence. Waving away a mosquito, Anya was no longer sure what she remembered.

"Alright," she said at last. "Let me get my suit, then."

Mel let out a shriek of glee as she ran straight into the dark water. Anya turned and shielded her eyes against the sun, half watching Mel splashing around and half watching for her eldest daughter.

On a rocky ridge far above her mother and sister, Christie took note of a faint series of imprints on the path before her. She crouched for a closer inspection, placing her hand next to one of them and spreading her fingers. Panting slightly from climbing the steep incline, she recalled what her mother had said about animal tracks, the difference between coyote and wildcat. These prints were large and wide, and she couldn't discern any claw marks. Did something move among the trees? Christie scanned the surroundings, breath catching in her throat. A cicada screamed. She held still, listening. Light and shadow danced among the ferns bending across the trail. A splash and a shriek startled her from below, followed by laughter as Mel plunged into the water and resurfaced again.

Her mother's voice: "Don't go too deep, okay?"

Christie stood, heart rabbiting in her chest. Glancing back in the direction of their camp, already obscured through the trees, she decided to continue on ahead. Just to see what was around the next bend.

My Father's Apiary

I walked through the sodden garden, boots squelching with each step, making my way to the chain-linked enclosure of my father's apiary. Between the cabin and the woods beyond, the six beehives were quiet under their black tarpapered wraps. With the vireos and thrushes finally returning to the north, it was time to unpack the bees from their deep-snow slumbers.

I held my breath as I knelt before each hive entrance. Tapping on the boxes with my knuckles, I listened for a buzzy response from within. Three of the six remained silent. My hands were unsteady as I ripped away the tarpaper in which my father had wrapped the hives the preceding autumn, and found that what I'd feared was true—half of his colonies hadn't made it through the winter. I started pulling the hives apart, removing empty frames and scraping away sticky black propolis and dead bees.

It happens every year. Some colonies don't make it through the winter, while others manage to thrive. I'd helped my father empty out dead hives countless times.

But this spring was different. Dad had died last autumn, leaving me with the question of what to do with his cabin, his apiary, and the surrounding woods. I couldn't think too far ahead yet. Instead, my task now was to clean out the dead hives and remove the old honeycomb before dividing the remaining bees and requeening them—and starting all over again.

>

The following morning, I came across a fawn and its mother in the woods. I was wielding rusty hedge clippers, trimming back the underbrush from the trail my father had maintained between the cabin and the river at the end of the property. A rustle in the underbrush, and I spotted a pair of wide, dark eyes. The fawn stood shakily as its mother moved to place herself between us. I waited till the breeze shifted, carrying my scent away, before continuing down the trail. When I looked back, the deer had disappeared among the spruces. Red squirrels were chasing each other raucously through the underbrush, and the warblers and sparrows were singing their hearts out about territory and sex. Such are the woods in spring.

I continued down to the river with the hedge clippers, snipping away. Several trees had fallen across the trail during the winter—I'd have to bring Dad's chainsaw next time to better clear the way. The trees thinned as I approached the slow-moving Muddy River, and the earthy forest floor gave way to smooth, Precambrian rock that sloped down into the water. I wiped sweat from my forehead with my sleeve and squinted across the river. It was narrower than I remembered. Some of the surrounding rock surfaces had shifted, and it was like seeing a friend's face after years of absence and being surprised to find that they've changed—which means, of course, that you've changed too. Trees that were barely saplings when I was a girl were fully grown, casting long shadows across the dark water. A lifetime ago, as a family, we used to come and pick wild raspberries from the tangled underbrush; we'd spread out a picnic lunch, swim and splash around, and doze in the sun.

A chipmunk nattered shrilly from somewhere nearby, and then there was only the whispering sound of the wind swaying the pines. Setting the hedge clippers aside, I squatted and splashed icy water on my face, savouring the river's familiar taste—earthy and metallic. Then, on a whim, I peeled off my clothes and took a running leap from the rocky bank.

The water was so cold that it was like jumping into a bed of knives. But as the shock subsided, I found the cold invigorating. After swimming a couple of laps from bank to bank, I unwound my tight bun and let my grey-brown hair fan out around my shoulders. I flipped over and drifted on my back, breasts bared to the sky. And that's when I had a sudden gut feeling that I was being watched.

I treaded water for a few moments, keeping only my eyes above the surface as I scanned the surrounding banks and forest beyond. Nothing was there, and nobody was in sight. My panic subsided, but the thrill had passed and my limbs were numbing. A group of ducks floated by, muttering among themselves as they passed. I front-crawled over to the bank and heaved myself out, badly scraping my forearm on a rock.

"Goddamn it." I splashed river water over the gash, already beading with blood, and pressed my palm against it to alleviate the throbbing pain.

Still naked, I let my skin air-dry and raked my fingers through my unruly hair. And that's when I noticed the black bear peering at me around the trunk of a nearby oak.

My hands instinctively flew to cover myself, as though the bear's small, dark gaze was that of a lurking voyeur. I scanned the surrounding area, hardly daring to move my head as I checked for a cub nearby. I didn't detect any other movement, but the bear was so close that I could hear the ragged huff of her breathing.

If I had taken two broad steps forward, I could have poked her in the nose.

She rose to her hind legs and snuffled the air as she scented me. I didn't do what you're supposed to do when faced with a black bear: *shout and wave your arms, make yourself look bigger, make lots of noise.* I didn't even have a can of bear spray on me— one of my father's cardinal rules. The hedge clippers, propped against a rock where I'd left them, were too far away to be of any use. I stood absolutely still, and waited for the bear to make the first move.

Finally, she made a noise somewhere between a snort and a grunt, and tossed her head before ambling back into the woods in the downstream direction. I didn't want to turn away. What if she came charging back? After a few breathless moments, I yanked on my jeans and damp t-shirt, ignoring the searing pain along my forearm, took up the hedge clippers and half walked, half jogged in the opposite direction—following my father's trail back up to the cabin.

>

If I was rattled by the encounter with the bear at the river, it was nothing compared to my surprise at finding a young man wandering through the woods the following afternoon.

I saw him before he saw me. I'd been clearing trails with my dad's old chainsaw, cutting up dead trees that were obstructing the way. This time, I'd remembered to hook a can of bear spray to my belt—just in case. As I finished bucking up the remains of a dead birch tree into stove lengths, the chainsaw began to splutter. I hit the chain brake, checked the choke, and pulled the cord. The machine wheezed, but it wouldn't restart.

"Oh come on," I muttered, yanking the cord again.

I gave up and braced myself against a nearby oak tree. My hands were shaking as I put the chainsaw down with a grunt. Maybe I should sell the property and return to my apartment in town. I couldn't handle the entire place on my own. Yet at forty-six years old—with my parents gone, my marriage long since dwindled into divorce, and motherhood having consisted of a handful of miscarriages—the old cabin, the garden, the bees, and even the surrounding forest somehow felt like the only family I had left.

I struggled to catch my breath, letting the tree hold my full weight. A couple of chickadees started up a chatty call-and-response conversation from a nearby bush and then abruptly fell silent.

A tall black-haired man wearing a red flannel shirt was wandering along the trail with a magnifying glass and a field notebook, heading my way. My hand went instinctively to the can of bear spray at my waist. Oblivious to my presence, he kneeled to examine a pile of deer scat on the trail, writing something down in a small notebook. He was young, I saw; maybe mid-to-late twenties. It was only when he reached my stack of birch logs that he stopped in his tracks, his gaze catching mine. Then his face lit up with sudden recognition.

"Professor Ladowsky!" he exclaimed.

I must have looked skeptical, because he rushed to introduce himself.

"It's Theo Rosgood. I took your class in college—four, maybe five years ago, I think."

I'd taught English classes at the local college for over a decade, and most twenty-something guys around town looked just about the same: shaggy hair, flannel shirt, scuffed-up jeans, and a kind of cocky self-assurance that's so exclusive to certain young men just before they start going bald.

"It was a good class," he was saying. "Couldn't quite keep up with all those Shakespearian soliloquies, though. Probably used SparkNotes for the term paper, to be honest."

"Sure," I said. "You and just about everybody else."

He gave me a sheepish grin.

"I heard the chainsaw going from way back by the river," he gestured over his shoulder with his magnifying glass. "Looks like you ran out of gas there."

I almost laughed out loud. An easy enough fix, after all. I should've known. I turned and busied myself with stacking the logs. Theo set his notebook and magnifying glass aside and grabbed a log in each hand, following my lead.

"Oh, you don't have to—" I began, pausing to smooth a strand of hair that had come loose from my bun.

But the truth was, I was grateful for the help. As we worked through the remaining logs, Theo explained that he was working as a wildlife biologist. He had a contract with the college lab for the summer and was currently creating an ecological report for the wilderness preserve that bordered my father's land.

"I must've wandered over the property line," he added, tearing a strip of peeling, paper-thin bark from a log before setting it on the pile.

There wasn't really a discernable property line that I knew of, except maybe on a creased map buried in some half-forgotten county filing cabinet. We finished stacking the final few logs. I wiped my forehead on my sleeve, revealing the new bandage on my forearm. It was itchy around the edges.

"Hey, what happened to your arm?" Theo asked, stepping closer.

"Bear encounter," I said, rubbing at the gauze. I could smell the tang of his aftershave. "By the river."

"No shit?"

I shrugged. Let him think whatever he wanted.

"Thanks for your help." I tugged my sleeve back down to my wrist. "Just make sure you stick to Crown land. This is private property."

"Sure thing, prof." He saluted me. "And if I come across a bear, I'll give you a holler."

I watched Theo stride down the trail until he disappeared around a bend. The smell of his aftershave lingered before fading into the forest's cedar tones, and I was alone again. I retrieved the chainsaw, slipped the bright-orange chain guard over the bar, and headed back to the cabin. At the tool shed I filled the chainsaw with fuel from one of Dad's jerry cans, trying to keep a steady hand as I poured. Then I went out and checked on the apiary, where the bees were foraging among the dandelions and other early bloomers.

I unhooked the gate and ventured into the enclosure, crouching before each hive and listening to the vibrating hum within until I was satisfied that they were doing well. As I leaned in closer, I caught a sweet, waxy fragrance around the entrance of one of the hives. The bright yellow dandelions brushing against my wrists reminded me that I hadn't been touched by a man in far longer than the turning of a long, cold season.

That night, my dreams were vivid and alive. Honey seeped through cracks in the walls, glistening in moonlight that poured in through the window. The entire cabin resonated with the bees' ancient, vibrating song as they drifted around me in slow motion. Warm honey pooled around my body, filling the bed. It was fragrant with wax, resin, and wildflowers. My mouth filled with the taste of nectar and pollen—sweet offerings from the bees.

And then I was dreaming of Theo Rosgood's hands tracing my skin in the dark.

➤

The next time I saw him, Theo was hanging over the apiary's chain-link fence and grinning at me—warm brown eyes lively, his wide jaw rough with dark stubble. He was wearing a green flannel shirt this time. I'd been so absorbed in looking for tiny eggs in the intricate honeycomb, a sign of a healthy, laying queen, that I hadn't paid attention to the roar of an engine coming down the distant country road or the swish of grass and crunch of gravel as he walked toward me.

"Morning!" he called out.

I was startled and then annoyed, uncomfortably aware that I had been murmuring to the bees as I worked alongside them. How long had he been there, watching me?

"Careful with the fence." I bent over the honeycomb again. "Haven't gotten around to reinforcing it."

Theo detached himself from the fence and came around to the gate. "Hey, you're a beekeeper, prof? That's cool."

"Listen, you don't have to call me professor or anything like that." I placed one wax frame back in the Langstroth hive and picked up another.

"What should I call you, then?"

When I said my first name, my voice came out sounding hoarse. I cleared my throat and repeated myself.

"Marika," he echoed, rolling it over his tongue. "May I come in?"

"Yeah, sure." I bent over the hive to replace the second frame, grateful for the bee veil I was wearing, the dark screen hiding my flushed face from view.

Theo unhooked the gate and stepped into the apiary. A smoky haze drifted between us as I fumbled with the bee smoker.

"This is incredible." He kneeled to watch a honeybee as she landed on a cluster of nearby white aster, the yellow pollen sacs on her hindlegs already bulging.

I turned back to the hive, closed the lid, and moved on to the next. Theo gazed around at the hand-painted hives and breathed in deeply—taking in the smouldering bee smoker as it blended with beeswax, wildflowers, and sweetness from the nearby herb garden.

"You painted these yourself?" He was admiring one of the compact Warré hives, which was painted with sprays of yellow clover.

"Yes," I said. I remembered how my father guided my paint-brush along the lines of a curling green vine. "Some of them."

All of the hives were painted with different patterns, images, and colour schemes. Each one had a placard on its roof, labeled with a name.

"What's with the names?" Still slightly wary of the bees, he squinted at the little wooden placards from a safe distance and recited, "*Andrejs, Agata, Lucija.*"

He stumbled over the foreign pronunciations, and I busied myself with refilling the bee smoker. The labels were something that Dad had started. After his own father had died, he buried the ashes under one of the hives and added a wooden label with *Andrejs* written in cursive. Then he buried his mother's ashes, so they could be together. Next, Mom's. Then, alone, I buried my father's cremains there. Under a fifth hive was a tiny, twelve-week fetus—my final miscarriage. The sixth hive was unnamed.

"Just names," I said, as I closed the bee smoker and aimed a few puffs at the hovering bees. "Family."

Then, bolder than most people unaccustomed to being around bees, he knelt before one of the Langstroth hives, closed his eyes, and listened to the reverberation of hundreds of thou-sands of tiny wings within. A worker bee landed on his bare arm, just below the rolled-up sleeve. Probing her way through the wiry hair, she was joined by a few of her curious sisters. In turn, Theo didn't swat them away. Clearly fascinated, he watched as they explored his skin until one by one, they flew off to continue foraging.

I finished adjusting the frames in a top-bar hive nearby and stepped back, removing my veil and emptying the charred innards of the bee smoker into the grass. Theo stood, brushing dirt from his knees, and asked if I wanted to go for a ride with him on his motorcycle.

I stared at him, bee veil dangling from my fist, and he gazed right back at me in earnest.

"You've got to be kidding me."

"I drove all this way to see you!" He shrugged. "And on my day off, too."

I set the veil on top of my mother's hive, labelled *Lucija*. I surprised myself by saying: "All right, let's go, then."

He lent me his helmet. Speeding recklessly along the country roads and hanging onto Theo Rosgood for dear life, I had more fun than I'd had in a long time.

The sun was setting when we got back to the cabin. I was wind burned and sore, but I invited him in. I started a small fire in the woodstove, and the narrow room soon filled with the scent of smoked cherry wood, beeswax, and crushed herbs. As we chatted about a motorcycle trip to the Yukon that he was planning for the end of the summer, I set two pieces of honeycomb on paper plates and poured thick cream over them. We started off with spoons, but polished off most of it with our fingers.

After stoking the fire, I brought out one of the last jars remaining from my father's buckwheat honey so that Theo could taste the difference from the golden clover variety we had just enjoyed. As I set the jar down on the table between us, he reached out and touched my hair

"Marika," he said. "You're beautiful."

He smelled like the woods—earthy, something like spruce or cedar. He dipped a fingertip into the honey jar, and raised it to my lips for me to suck clean.

➤

I saw Theo nearly every day that summer. I hadn't adjusted my schedule around someone else's for longer than I'd care to admit, but our time together settled into a natural rhythm. He went to the college lab during the weekdays, then came by the cabin in the late afternoons with an offering—books on forest plants and bee biology, cans of kerosene, a chainsaw sharpener kit, or a framed black-and-white photo he took of me in my father's apiary. We often went animal tracking through the woods, on account of his fieldwork.

Some nights, we built a great bonfire in the clearing behind the cabin, the flames reaching taller than a grown woman toward the sky. It would burn all night, and we'd fall asleep there in the pile of blankets we laid out, half-naked and exposed to the stars. We'd waken, slick with dew and the fire still smoking a trail to the pale sky and the fading moon.

One thundery night, I woke in a sudden sweat. I'd grown so used to our nights outdoors that being surrounded by four rigid walls was stifling. Theo lay beside me, his deep sleep somehow undisturbed by the rain pounding on the tin roof above us. I got up and went to the outhouse. As I made my way back to the cabin, the skin on my arms and the back of my neck prickled. Pausing, I sensed movement nearby as I cast the wan beam of the flashlight over the tool shed and apiary fence.

A strike of lightning briefly illuminated the clearing, followed by a thundering crack that sent me stumbling back to the cabin, where I crawled back into bed beside Theo. I couldn't shake the feeling that there had been a presence nearby, alert and aware, observing me in the dark.

The following morning, we discovered that a bear had ransacked the apiary during the night—sometime during or after the storm. It had managed to climb the fence, which had split and toppled into a mess of splintered wood and twisted wire. Broken frames and clawed-up honeycombs were strewn through the damp grass, already crawling with ants. Bees were humming around the devastated hives, flying low and hovering, recongregating on the destroyed honeycombs. Some hives had been knocked over and purposefully pried open, their interiors exposed as the bear indulged in a feast of dripping honeycomb. There were bloodstains on the hive boxes, along with tufts of black fur. The bear had injured itself upon entering the apiary in its unceremonious way.

I pulled on a pair of sheepskin gloves and handed Theo a bee veil, then hopped over the broken fence. I hesitated, briefly overwhelmed by a sickly sweet smell that infused the enclosure—the scent of communal honeybee fear, released as an alarm signal into the air. I murmured soothingly to the bees as I got to work. After a few moments I glanced back at Theo, who was still standing by the fence. I gestured to the strewn Langstroth boxes and instructed him to help me with the heavy lifting. Obediently, he went over to the boxes and put a tentative hand on an overturned honey super. Bees swarmed all around us.

"Don't worry too much about being stung," I said as calmly as I could. "Most of the bees from that one are gone—see?" A cluster of bees had formed among the branches of a nearby maple. "The queen is among them. They'll start scouting for a safe space to take her—a new place to live."

Theo stacked the fractured hive bodies, then moved on to straighten a top-bar hive that had been knocked over. We worked efficiently, speaking in low tones or with hand gestures, the restoration of the apiary taking the greater part of the morning and into the early afternoon. We salvaged honeycomb wherever possible, sorting out broken frames from those that were still functional. We set up a temporary enclosure, using as much of the wood and wire as we could. Gradually, some of the hovering bees started returning home to investigate. Only two of the six hives appeared to be missing queens, which was nothing short of a miracle.

"What will happen to the bees from the colonies without queens?" Theo asked as he placed the final box atop a stocky Langstroth hive, its boxes painted with roses and vines.

"If we're lucky, they'll join up with one of the other colonies." I pressed the lid onto the hive. "Bees don't like strangers in their homes, but they rarely turn away a worker bee who arrives with honey or pollen to contribute to the colony."

To retrieve the swarm that had retreated to the nearby maple tree, I instructed Theo to bring over an empty top-bar hive from the shed. We set it up nearby with its lid tilted open, and I placed a handful of rosemary and lavender from my father's garden inside the box, alongside some honeycomb that we had scraped free of ants.

"They'll have scout bees out looking for a new home," I said. "The smell of the herbs might draw them in."

Theo went into the cabin and returned a few moments later with two ice-cold beers. We pulled up a couple of lawn chairs and settled near the apiary to watch the buzzing activity around the hives. A robin was offering its late-summer evening song from a low branch of the maple; the forest beyond was otherwise hushed and still.

"They really mean something to you, eh, these bees," Theo said.

I opened my mouth to respond, then pressed my lips together. There was a roaring sound growing ever louder in my ears, until it was reverberating through my entire body—I wasn't sure if I could hold myself together for much longer. After a few deep breaths I realized that the sound wasn't coming from somewhere within me, after all, but rather from the bees clustered in the maple tree. In one coordinated motion, they all rose in a swarm before swirling across the clearing to the open hive that we had set up for them. Neither of us moved, even as the roar died down and was replaced by the tremulous stillness that precedes late-summer dusk.

I choked back a sob. I had almost lost them—my father's hives, my honeybees. Theo reached over and put an arm around me as I steadied myself, which took some time. Then I walked over to the newly occupied hive, murmuring in my usual way as I tapped the lid shut.

➤

The summer dipped into autumn, shifting closer to the time of the honey harvest. The bees continued to forage among the goldenrod and the last of the late-summer wildflowers, but I knew that the hives wouldn't produce much honey this season. The bees would be focused on trying to produce enough stores to survive another long winter.

Apples ripened at the edge of my father's garden, and wild mushrooms clustered along the forest trail. Theo's contract with the college ended, and his motorcycle trip to the Yukon was approaching.

"What are you planning to do out there?" I asked him one afternoon as we stacked logs in the woodshed behind the cabin.

"I don't know yet, really." He handed me two logs, and I arranged them on the sizeable pile we had already built up. "Maybe tree planting or volunteering on an organic farm for a while."

I stacked more wood, trying to remember what I'd been doing when I was twenty-seven. Finishing my graduate program. Planning my wedding, preparing for a future that hadn't quite turned out the way I'd imagined it would.

"Enjoy it," I said, pausing to brush loose hair from my eyes with my gloved hand. "Whatever you end up doing, enjoy the hell out of it."

He passed me another couple of logs. "Would you come with me?"

Something of the wild girl I never quite was stirred within me, if only for a fleeting moment. But I was too old now to uproot my entire life for a man. I thanked him sincerely for the offer, telling him that ten years ago a version of myself might have said yes. I'd decided to spend the winter at the cabin, rather than going back to town. Theo nodded, glancing behind us at the apiary. The colourful hives stood out from the dark backdrop of the forest, and the sun was already sinking below the treeline.

"I get it," he said. "If I had a place of my own like this, I wouldn't leave either."

The day after Theo left for the Yukon, I wrapped the beehives in what remained of the black tarpaper from the toolshed. The nearby woods were hushed, almost silent, at that time of year. I took my time and insulated the colonies with extra Styrofoam. My hands were steady as I used the staple gun to pin down a double layer of tarpaper. It was the best I could do to help the bees survive another long winter.

Wolff Island

Martin mutters to himself as he peers through the fog at the empty road and dense woods just beyond the gravel shoulder. His car windows are rolled down on both sides, letting in mosquitoes and drizzling rain. He inches along before he comes to a rolling stop and pulls the handbrake. He removes his steamed-up glasses. They haven't been gone for longer than—what, maybe ten minutes? Twenty? But he wasn't paying attention, and now he doesn't know how long he's been waiting for his wife and son to return from the woods.

He hits the horn twice. The first honk sounds like a startled animal crying out, the second like a mournful bleat. He switches the car off, puts his glasses back on, and gets out. He stomps across the waterlogged ditch, resenting that he has to wander around in the raw weather as he calls Tim's name. Why in hell is he shouting for his two-year-old son and not his wife? He scans the edge of the bush, but there's no trace of them. Not even a footprint. He's no longer even sure that he's in the right spot anymore. It could have been right here, or maybe just over there, that they slipped into the woods. It all looks the same—

cedars, spruces, underbrush—everything just blends together in the fog.

Martin stumbles over an exposed root and loses his footing in the wet grass. Pain sears up through his calf from his ankle.

"Shit!" He hobbles back to the car and drops into the driver's seat with the door open to the rain, leg extended as he rips open a bag of beef jerky. No other vehicles pass as he waits. It's still early in the season for camping, so there are few visitors on Wolff Island. Martin and his wife chose the island specifically for its remote location. They drove seven and a half hours north from the city, enjoying the landscape's slow shift from mixed-wood plains into boreal forest. But they hadn't anticipated the steady rain that just wouldn't let up, or the thick fog that rolled endlessly in from the lake.

Martin hefts his sodden leg in and shuts the door. Another ten minutes drag by with no sign of their return. He removes his glasses again and pinches the bridge of his nose. Earlier that morning they'd gone to the visitor centre, where he'd lingered over an informational plaque mounted in front of a life-sized habitat diorama. There aren't any major predators on Wolff Island, it said, but the island, which encompasses an area of approximately 120 square kilometres of rough, rocky terrain, is home to some of the largest moose in North America. He read that, throughout the past decade or so, the local moose population has been rehabilitated after a significant decline caused by a spike in development in the surrounding region. By the coming winter, when the lake freezes over, the moose will be able to migrate across to the mainland and resume their role in the natural order of things.

The repopulation seemed reassuring to Martin, as he moved to stand before an enormous stuffed moose with massive antlers and black marble eyes. This was an optimistic story about the environment for once, conveying a sense of hope that humans had seen the error of their ways and were redeeming themselves through the skillful application of concrete science. Smart, qualified people could repair this particular little fuck-up, and the woodland ecosystem would be whole once again.

Next to the moose, there was a donation box where visitors could contribute to ongoing wildlife research on the island. When he noticed the petite blonde cashier looking in his general direction, Martin slipped a five-dollar bill through the slot. His wife was drawn by a sudden piercing wail emitted by their son, who had crawled over to the adjacent gift shop. Tim had his heart set on a small stuffed salamander and was sobbing as his mother knelt next to him, gently tugging it away. She spoke in cool, soothing tones that never quite succeeded in conferring good reason onto the toddler. Martin had lingered by the display moose until his wife had hissed at him and jerked her head towards the exit, their red-faced son squirming in her arms as he grieved for the forbidden salamander.

After his wife took Tim out to the car, Martin picked up a free pamphlet about the island and purchased a can of insect repellant and a package of beef jerky from the cashier, along with the salamander. He knew the stuffed toy would cause a fuss—his wife was always complaining that he was too indulgent. She claimed that Tim had to learn that he couldn't simply acquire everything he could get his hands on. But Martin didn't see how a toy here or a candy bar there could cause much harm. He figured the rest of the kid's life would be an exercise in unsatisfied desires and self-denial, anyway.

Back in the car, his wife had given him a cold look when he handed the salamander to the boy. Then she turned away, and they settled into a steely silence as Martin backed the car out of the parking lot. Only Tim seemed happy, his tantrum dwindling into a gurgle as he tugged at one of the salamander's black button eyes. Martin smirked over at his wife, but she was facing the passenger's side window—gazing fixedly at the white wall of fog, at nothing at all.

Not wanting to return to their dismal campsite, Martin decided to drive around the island so they could take in what the pamphlet promised were unforgettable views of the rugged coastline. However, the fog was so dense that they could see little beyond a few metres in any given direction, as if there were nothing but the dirt road and impenetrable bush all around them. Tim started fussing again, tossing the salamander aside and whining about having to pee. Martin's wife rummaged around in her bag and pulled out a picture book called *The Woodland ABC*. She twisted around in her seat to try and entertain Tim.

Martin felt himself shrinking away from their surroundings as they drove on. He had a crick in his neck and his shoulders sagged, as though something grim were slowly pressing them down.

➤

A mosquito whines around Martin's left ear. He gnaws at the last of the jerky, finally swallowing it down, and then scrolls through his contacts with a greasy fingertip until he taps on a photo of his wife. It takes a few moments for the line to connect—the island is just barely within range of any sort of signal. It rings once, twice, and then the call drops. The mosquito stings his earlobe and Martin slaps at it absently.

He glances back at his son's car seat—crumbs in the sticky creases, the new salamander lying belly-up on the black fabric. Tim had managed to partway pull out its eye, which stares glassily back at him as it dangles from a thread. *The Woodland ABC* is open to a two-page spread of a pastoral scene featuring a silly looking moose against a bushy backdrop. *M is for Moose, the mightiest of herbivores.*

As Tim's fussing had risen to a piercing shriek, his wife had tossed the book aside and told Martin to pull over so she could take the boy into the bush to pee. Martin had obeyed, annoyed. Couldn't the kid wait till they got to one of the park's public washrooms? She pulled open the back door, shouldered the backpack, and unbuckled Tim from his seat. *We'll be a few minutes*, she said as she zipped up the toddler's rain jacket before pulling on her own. *I have to go, too.* After she pushed both doors shut with her hip, mother and son turned and walked hand-in-hand into the woods. That was the last Martin had seen of them.

>

It's two o'clock. He tries calling his wife again, but all he gets is an automated message telling him that the customer he has dialed is not available.

Not knowing what else to do, he drives to the gatehouse. Reluctantly, he asks the park warden if his wife and son have shown up. He tries to make a joke of it, *Either they're lost or I am!* When he adds that they have been missing for over three hours, during which time there was a brief but severe thunderstorm, the warden gets a serious look and leads Martin into the staffroom. He settles down at the table and takes out a small notebook, asking Martin to paint a detailed picture of the past few hours.

The family had woken early that morning, Martin explains, after not having slept much, on account of the unfamiliar surroundings and the rocky ground where they'd pitched their tent. His wife had managed to get a smoky fire going to warm up some water for instant coffee and oatmeal before it started pissing rain again. Tim had started whining about being cold. When they finally piled into the car to go kill some time at the visitor centre, it was around 10:30 a.m.

Martin shuts his eyes, trying to recall the number glowing on the dash. He hadn't checked the time or picked up his phone when they went into the bush. After all, that had been the whole point of the camping trip—to escape from their cramped urban condo, to get offline and spend some quality time together as a family. It was his wife's idea.

Prompted by the warden, Martin says his wife is wearing a sweatshirt emblazoned with the crest of her alma mater. He's pretty sure of it, as she often wears that sweatshirt. University of Toronto, he clarifies, and the sweatshirt is dark green. Or is it black? With jeans and black rubber boots, he adds, closing his eyes as he puts the picture together in his mind. She had a pink Gore-Tex jacket. Tim's wearing a blue rain jacket and red rubber boots with a yellow stripe, he says with more certainty. Or maybe yellow with a red stripe? He hesitates again, and the warden's pen hovers over the notebook. Martin states that the boots are red with a yellow stripe, and the jacket is definitely blue—some kind of pale blue-greenish. The warden nods and tucks his notes away.

"Not to worry," he says, businesslike. "No one's ever gone missing on Wolff Island."

Martin wipes sweat from his brow with his sleeve, heartened that sensible professionals are taking over the situation. Of course his wife and son aren't missing. They're just lost, and that's different. There's been a little misunderstanding, a missed connection somewhere. They went into the bush at one little gap in the trees, and emerged somewhere else by accident—maybe just as he'd started inching the car away. It's not his fault. The fog made a blur of everything, and they had lost sight of one another. The warden nods along to Martin's rambling. Yes, he agrees, it's the sort of thing that could happen.

➤

To Martin, the park warden and his pretty, redheaded assistant look like teenagers. He's pressing an ice pack against his ankle. The redhead brought it for him when she noticed him limping. Turns out she's a summer student at the park, and the warden's still in college. It's 5:51 p.m. He's checking his phone obsessively now.

Martin repeats his story to them both, gratified by the redhead's wide-eyed sympathy and her almost teary concern for his little son. All the same, they seem energized by the situation. Clearly not much happens on Wolff Island. He and the warden head out in the park's pickup truck, circling the entire island twice. Martin points out their campsite and shows him where they stopped on the island's single dirt road. He also identifies the gap in the trees where he's fairly certain he last saw them. The warden gets out of the truck and ties bright orange trail markers at both spots before they drive back to the gatehouse.

Rain pelts against the only window in the room. Martin checks his phone. No messages. He tries calling his wife again, but after a few rings he hangs up.

There's a distant roll of thunder, and he sees the warden and the redhead exchange a worried glance. But his wife has common sense, Martin believes. Even she would say that it was better if she got lost instead of him. Soon enough, he thought, she would show up, soaking wet and half carrying, half dragging their sniffling son with her, furious at Martin for having left them behind. He must have overlooked something along the way, something obvious. Or she could be trying to teach him a lesson of some kind. Maybe she'd noticed him looking at the cashier in the visitor centre. He imagines his wife emerging from the bush just as the police are called in, raising her eyebrows at his having made a big deal of the little hike she'd decided to take on her own. Making a fool of him.

The warden and the girl are going out to search the island again. It's decided that Martin will stay at the gatehouse because of his sore ankle, and in case his wife and son show up. The warden also points out that cell reception is more reliable there, so Martin can continue to try and reach her—or maybe she'll try to reach him. The girl brings him a bottle of water, a Styrofoam cup of acidic coffee, and three packets each of sugar and cream before heading out. Through the streaked window, Martin watches as the truck melts away into the pouring rain.

He examines a plaque on the wall, emblazoned with a vintage version of the provincial park logo and the name *Wolff Island*. It starts to annoy him, that spelling. *Wolff*. He mutters the word to himself, extending the final consonant until he runs out of breath. He shakes his head and takes a sip of coffee, still glaring at the plaque. At least the double "f" makes it clear that the island is named after a person and not the animal. A historical figure, most likely. Some intrepid general who reclaimed the island from the conniving French or grasping Americans during a distant war—after the territory had been stolen and chopped up into imperial quarters in the first place.

The coffee's gone cold. Martin takes another sip. The stuff tastes foul. He glances at the nearby wall clock. 9:15 p.m. For the first time since entering the gatehouse, he notices how noisily the clock grinds its gears, measuring time out in tiny increments. *Tick, tick, tick,* alternating with the *drip, drip, drip* of rain at the window. He removes his glasses and rubs his eyes. Then he sinks forward, his head between his arms, forehead pressed to the table.

Martin is still face down when the park warden returns nearly two hours later.

"Uh, sir?" His uniform is thoroughly drenched, as though he decided to go for a swim in the lake.

Martin sits up. There's no sign of the redhead. Overtime must be above her pay grade. He puts his glasses back on, disappointed. The warden explains that he's contacted the police over on the mainland.

"Technically, we're supposed to wait twenty-four hours to report something like this," he says, switching off the lights at intervals as they head down the corridor. "But since there's a child involved, I decided to call it in early."

"What should I do?" Martin asks.

"Well, I'm going to keep patrolling the area. Why don't you go back to the campsite, in case they show up there?"

Martin nods and thanks him, then checks his phone. 11:03 p.m., no signal. His ankle throbs as he shuffles after the warden, who takes his number and promises to keep him informed. The warden locks up the gatehouse and they head off in opposite directions through the murky night. The rain's mostly let up, but there's a lingering raw chill in the air.

Back at the campsite, Martin circles the perimeter with his smartphone's flashlight. Scanning the wet leaves and tangled underbrush, he finds one of Tim's socks, red and sodden, which the boy had thrown aside during a tantrum that morning. Tossing it onto the picnic table, he polishes off a half-eaten granola bar his wife had left behind at breakfast. Then, after struggling with the tent's tricky zipper, he finally heaves himself through the elf-sized entrance.

The sleeping bags are surprisingly dry, so he wriggles fully-clothed into the largest one. The pillow smells of his wife's sickly sweet hair products. He replaces it with Tim's firetruck-patterned cushion before switching off the flashlight and zipping the sleeping bag up to his throat. There's no difference between closing his eyes and keeping them wide open. The darkness beyond the tent seethes and clicks with insect noises; the surrounding forest is a chorus of drips and whispers.

Martin drifts for a while until he finally slips deeper into sleep. At the junction of late night and early morning, he's wakened with a jolt by the sound of snuffling around the tent. He lays rigidly in his sleeping bag. He hears a grunt, followed by the sound of damp leaves being compressed underfoot. There are no wolves here, he reminds himself, and no bears either. There's nothing left to fear on Wolff Island.

➤

The police officer arrives at the gatehouse before dawn, with a search-and-rescue dog on a stout leash. Martin is drinking coffee with the warden. Reassurance washes over him as he looks at the German Shepherd, who assumes an alert, ready-and-waiting stance next to his handler. The officer takes her time listening to Martin's story, repeating certain questions in different ways and taking notes. She then compares her notes with those the warden jotted down the previous night.

Martin's palms are sweaty, and his back aches from sleeping on rocky ground. The officer puts the pillowcase used by Martin's wife into a plastic bag—something for the dog to get her scent from when they arrive at the spot where Martin last saw them.

The officer nods briskly in Martin's direction before heading out, which he interprets as a subtle way of conveying that the situation is under control. When she's in the corridor, he over-hears her telling the warden that finding any kind of trail through the bush will be a challenge after yesterday's downpour. Martin glances at his phone's battery reading, which has dropped to twenty per cent. He pulls a charging cable from his pocket and plugs his phone into the outlet beside the coffee machine. It's 7:12 a.m.

By noon, they've brought in a helicopter. He can hear it chop-chopping in the middle distance, and the sound puts him on edge. He's sitting in the gatehouse with the warden, who's sucking down his third cup of weak coffee. The police dog, its drenched fur now towel dried, is dozing on the floor like somebody's pet. The officer hasn't spoken to Martin since she returned, letting the warden operate as her intermediary.

Martin wonders if he's beginning to look like a suspect or something. That's how it happens in the movies. They'll start thinking that he did his family in or left them behind on purpose somewhere. He sits perfectly still, with what he hopes is an inno-cent but concerned expression on his face. He's only half listening as the warden starts telling them about the rising water level in the surrounding lake.

"Commercial boat traffic increases every year, eh," the warden explains, raising his voice as the coffee machine grinds out another cup. "It's actually *quadrupled* in the past few years, can you imagine? It's causing all sorts of problems, one of them being unprecedented erosion."

The gist of what he's saying is that the island is slowly being scoured away, sinking flake by flake into the choppy, slate-grey water. The officer's walkie-talkie crackles to life, and the sudden blare of static and muffled voices nearly startles the cup from Martin's hand. As she strides from the room, he can't help but notice how her uniform nicely emphasizes her hips. He watches furtively through the window as she speaks into the device, admiring her silky blonde ponytail. Then she disappears into the fog as she crosses the parking lot towards the visitor centre, which is just barely discernible through the impermeable grey.

Martin unplugs his phone and opens the photo app. He has only a handful of pictures from their trip so far, mostly documenting a few small-town monuments on their long drive up from the city. Their son had shrieked with glee as they drove the car onto the ferry, and they managed to snap a few family selfies from the deck with the misty island as a backdrop. They wore matching blue plastic ponchos, but the three of them didn't quite fit in the frame—in one photo, Martin is entirely cut out; in another, only his wife's shoulder and frizz of her hair are visible. Tim's face is a blur in both shots because he wouldn't stop squirming. Martin swipes back and forth through the images and feels his throat constrict.

"Look," he says hoarsely to the warden, who's been fiddling with the coffee machine. "Look, here we are. This is us."

The warden sets a Styrofoam cup before him and gives Martin's shoulder a squeeze before leaving the room again. 2:30 p.m. Martin slips his phone into his pocket. He gets up and takes the coffee outside, still favouring his sore ankle. Outside, the air is thick with moisture. He takes a deep breath, filling his lungs. Briefly, he has the sensation of having gills—of breathing underwater. He rubs his neck and steadies himself by taking a sip of coffee. He nearly chokes as a shadowy figure rises from the fog.

She seems alien to him at first. Only her head looms through the dense grey surroundings, disembodied, floating across the parking lot. Her eyes are alert, dark, intelligent. He hears the faintest crunch as she steps onto the gravel. She doesn't seem to notice him until he shifts his weight off his bad ankle, and she freezes at the sound of his foot scuffing the ground. Martin holds his breath, transfixed. He stares at her, and she surveys him with a steady gaze. Her long face is expressionless. There's a shuffling sound and a second head appears through the haze—a paler, smaller version of the mother, unsteady on its spindly legs.

She makes a snuffling noise, a familiar grunt. He recalls his mysterious nighttime visitor, and thinks—*it was them.*

The moose and her calf have vanished into the thick air and spitting rain. He waits, heart pounding and ears straining. They were so close one moment, and then gone the next.

He's about to head back into the gatehouse when he hears approaching voices. The mist is thicker than ever, and it looks as though it might begin to rain in earnest again. He recognizes the officer's husky tone and the warden's slight drawl.

"Double-checked with the ferry operator, too," the officer is saying. "It would be hard to miss them. Not many people going back and forth this time of year—especially with this weather."

"You can't go missing on this island," the warden says, almost irritated. "It isn't big enough. I guess the chopper couldn't see much through the fog?"

"It lifted mid-morning," the officer replies. "Just briefly, but we were able to fly over the entire island."

A lengthy pause follows. Martin imagines the helicopter looping around, a relentless, all-seeing eye taking everything in.

"If you ask me," the officer says, "the only way to go missing around here is by not wanting to be found."

The gatehouse door creaks open, then shut again. Martin reaches out to steady himself, but his fingers grasp at nothing—

at the fog, at the air. The ground seems to loosen and soften under his feet. He hears the slow, rhythmic lapping of waves. The island, pressed down by the weight of fog, is gently crumbling into the unseen lake. Rain drives down hard, and harder still. Martin feels the land pitch and give way beneath him—earth and rock shifting and sinking as they dissolve, becoming water.

The Best Little Hunter

E velyn had been roaming the damp woods since well before
dawn, but she wasn't having any luck with the turkeys this
year. She and her father had done the spring hunt together for
as long as she could remember, and this forested hill, which they
called the Mountain, was one of their favourite spots. They could
usually flush out a few turkeys roosting in the early mornings,
toms and hens alike. But Evelyn had just moved her father into
the old folks' home in nearby Sadowa, and at thirty-eight years
old, this was the first year she was doing the hunt alone.

Confident in her skills as a solo hunter, she had prepared
everything she needed well in advance—the gear, the decoys,
preplanned hunting locations, and a few new slate calls. But she
hadn't seen much evidence of turkeys around the Mountain at
all. Instead, she'd found plenty of signs of coyotes—paw prints,
clumps of scat filled with seeds, bone fragments, and what
appeared to be the shredded bits of a cat's collar.

As she squatted to examine another greyish mound of coyote
scat on the trail, a distant shot rang out from somewhere in the
surrounding woods—maybe on the other side of the Mountain.

Evelyn stood. Maybe other hunters were having better luck. Her back ached and her nose was running from the early-morning chill. It was time to call it a day.

After hiking out of the woods, she slung the decoys into the back of her truck, peeled off her muddy camo jacket, and packed up her shotgun. It took three tries to get the pickup started, and even then it was running rough. Just as she pulled out from the gravel shoulder, a quarry truck came around the bend with a bellowing honk and Evelyn had to swerve hard to just avoid veering off into the ditch.

There was a lump of fur on the side of the road as she rounded the bend. Too small for a wolf, too large for a fox, too lean for a dog—the broken body must be a coyote. The trucker hadn't been honking at her, then, but at the animal that had darted across his path.

Evelyn considered driving on and leaving the carcass behind. She was still shivering from the cold. But the coyote's appearance seemed prophetic somehow. That very week, a town hall meeting was held about coyotes at the local pub, co-hosted by the Sadowa Hunting Club—she was the current president—and the local Wildlife Services Centre. The meeting addressed the recent spike in local coyote incidents. Somebody's cat had disappeared; some-one else's dog got badly bitten. Another dog birthed a litter of pups that had distinct coyote features—long snouts, and some-thing about the yellow eyes.

At the meeting, the discussion about general safety tips had been overridden by a heated debate about whether coyote hunting should be temporarily deregulated in order to rein in the excess population. Evelyn herself had taken the stance of at least considering deregulation as an option, though Nicholai, the wildlife services officer, had insisted that killing a coyote or two would not cut back their numbers. Coyotes are territorial, he explained, so if a few were removed here and there, others would just move in to claim their own place. Evelyn had pointed out that the robustness of the coyote population was exactly why opening the hunting season should be considered.

The debate had yielded no definite conclusions. In the end, everyone went home with Sadowa Hunting Club promotional stickers in one hand and a *Coyote Safety Tips* brochure in the other.

Evelyn left the truck running as she got out to inspect the roadkill. It was a young male. A pair of coyotes had been singing that very morning as she sat half-frozen in the early spring rain, covered in dead leaves and waiting for turkeys. Now, as she kneeled to take a closer look, the coyote's chest rose and fell almost imperceptibly.

Gravel crunched under her boots as she stepped back, not wanting to be face to face with him if he turned out to just be stunned. His breathing was shallow and irregular, and blood was seeping into the half-frozen dirt. She peered into the woods— maybe his mate was nearby. Coyotes often mated for life, and early spring was right around the time they started denning down together.

When she looked down at him again, the coyote's amber eye was open and pinned right on her. Evelyn froze, and answered with an involuntary sound low in her throat. The coyote made a whining noise, followed by a huffed exhalation of breath. His eye was unblinking. Half-blinded as he must be by shock and pain, she was unsure whether the coyote could actually see her. But she couldn't look away.

The call of a crow—three hoarse syllables—was echoed in eerie succession by others nearby. The scavengers were gathering. Evelyn hesitated, thinking about her shotgun in the truck. She wished someone else was around to make the decision for her. With a heavy tread she went to retrieve the gun, breaking the action open and loading a shell into the chamber. Bolting it shut, she returned to the coyote and found that the amber eye had glazed over.

Evelyn disarmed the gun. Then she knelt and hovered a hand over the body, closing her eyes and absorbing the warmth as it ebbed.

➤

In town, Evelyn sorted through a handful of change as Sue, a cousin on her father's side and ten years her junior, rang up her order for two large coffees—one black, the other with double cream and double sugar—at the drive-thru window. They chatted about coyotes and the piss-poor hunting weather.

"No luck so far?" Sue asked, sorting the coins into the register. "Jason and the twins haven't seen much, either. He says it's because there's too many coyotes, you know? Taking all the turkeys for themselves."

"Yeah," Evelyn shrugged. "Guess they gotta eat, too."

"Sure they do, little bastards," Sue grinned, firing a mock shot with her thumb and forefinger. "Jason takes a crack at them whenever he can, eh."

"Right," Evelyn said.

Sue's husband was the kind of trigger-happy hunter Evelyn tried to avoid. She resisted asking Sue whether Jason had acquired the necessary tags that would permit him to legally shoot coyotes. She eyed an oversized Ford Silverado pulling up behind her in the rear-view mirror.

"Anyway, I'll throw in a muffin for you—we've got overstock, and I'll just end up eating them all myself. You're looking awfully thin these days, you know. So jealous." Sue rested a hand on her belly, plump and expectant. "This one's got me craving sweets like crazy. Jason thinks it's a girl this time."

"Mmm," Evelyn said, accepting the warm paper bag.

"And how's Uncle Walt?" Sue asked.

"He's doing fine, I guess. Not too great, you know, but fine."

Sue nodded, pursing her lips as she passed Evelyn the coffee tray. "Maybe we'll pay him a little visit, the boys and me, once he's all settled in. You just let me know."

"Sure, I bet he'd appreciate that."

"It's sad, really," Sue sighed, her still hand draped over her belly, "that he won't get to hold a grandbaby of his own."

Evelyn was relieved of the immediate need to respond to Sue by a honk from the Silverado, which had pulled right up to her back bumper. Sue rolled her eyes and waved Evelyn off, calling after her:

"The baby shower's on Saturday—I'll message you the details, all right?"

Evelyn sped through town. She steadied herself as she waited at the only intersection, using a handful of napkins to wipe spilled coffee from the front of her jacket. Until recently, people used to say, *don't worry, there's still time.* She used to secretly seethe. Such remarks were becoming less frequent, and in turn, her ambivalence about motherhood had settled into acquiescence; it was something else she didn't need reminding of, as time gradually made the decision for her. It was only recently that she'd started feeling vague stirrings of something like regret—now that her mother was gone and her father was fading into early-onset dementia, she faced the prospect of no longer being anyone's daughter herself.

Evelyn parked in front of the Sadowa Town Library, which also served as the headquarters of the Wildlife Services Centre and the Sadowa Hunting Club. She'd been a card-carrying member of the club since she was old enough to hold a rifle steady, and although the president gig was really more of an administrative role, it offered a modest salary and enough flexibility to tend to her father as needed. Evelyn pulled off her toque and smoothed the static from her limp blonde hair. Carrying the coffee tray in both hands with the muffin bag perched on top, she closed the pickup's door with her hip. In the foyer, Nicholai was taking down the printed notices they had tacked up for the coyote meeting.

"No hard feelings, eh?" he said, referring to their opposing stances during the debate.

"Never." Evelyn handed him the double cream, double sugar from the tray. She also offered him Sue's overstock muffin, which he accepted with a friendly wink.

The fact was that the Sadowa Hunting Club was one of the main financial supporters of Wildlife Services Centre, which largely operated by donations; thirty percent of every club membership went directly to them. Despite certain differences in perspective, the interests of the two organizations were aligned on environmental concerns and issues of conservation.

Nicholai gestured at the bulletin board in front of them as he took a sip.

"Still gets me every time," he said, with a sly smile.

Evelyn glanced at the row of old Polaroids and grimaced. Her own childish face grinned back at her from each photo, under the heading: *Sadowa's Best Little Hunter!* At seven-and-a-half years old, she had been the youngest resident of Sadowa to success-fully bag a turkey—the first of the season that year. In the photo, she was holding a tom, nearly her own size, by its feet with both hands. She was grinning, one of her front teeth missing. Other photos featured Evelyn at almost-twelve with her first buck, a six-pointer; then at thirteen, squatting next to a bull moose.

"I'm going to take those down, I swear," she said. "They're ancient, anyway."

"Nah, you can't," Nicholai said, with a laugh. "Seeing as you're still the local record holder."

Evelyn rolled her eyes at him. A phone rang in the Wildlife Services office, and he gave her a salute before jogging off to answer it.

"Hey, Nic," she called after him. "There's a dead coyote on the quarry road, out by the bridge. Maybe you should go take a look."

"Right on," he said. "I'll get the crew on it."

As he disappeared into his office, Evelyn glanced up at the bulletin board again. The final photo, which was partially obscured by a town hall notice, featured her at fourteen, with a mouth full of braces, standing next to the bulk of a black bear. She was standing with her shotgun crooked in her elbow, her father bending over her with his arm around her shoulders, and their old hound Maisy sitting on her haunches in front of them. Kids at school had called Evelyn the Bear Killer after that, something her father insisted she should be proud of. He had showed her how to skin and tan it, and now the hide was draped over a chair in Evelyn's mobile home at the edge of town.

Evelyn turned her back on the photos, heading down the hall to the office across from Nicholai's. She straightened the Sadowa Hunting Club sign hanging on the door before closing it behind her.

>

The following morning, Evelyn returned to the woods as early as she could drag herself out of the house. She'd had another restless night—up half the time pacing, the other half dreaming of the coyote's amber eye staring at her. When she finally woke for good at 4:00 a.m., it was because she thought she'd heard her mother's voice saying her name, calling her awake.

Crows scattered as she pulled up to the bloody spot where the coyote had breathed his last—Nicholai's crew had removed the body, but some tufts of bloodied fur clung to the gravel. Evelyn left the truck parked at the side of the road, pulled her toque low over her eyes, slung her shotgun over her shoulder, and made her way through a narrow gap in the spruces. Snow still lingered in the thickest parts of the bush as she moved up the Mountain, but green shoots were already pushing up elsewhere. Mist sifted through the trees, rendering the familiar woods secretive and strange. Evelyn glanced behind her, feeling watched.

At a sudden flicker of wings, she raised the shotgun—but it was only an owl on its way to roost.

Evelyn stooped to examine glossy pellets of deer scat on the leaf litter. She arranged herself among the exposed roots of an oak tree on a rocky incline. Pressing her spine to the trunk, she put the turkey caller to her mouth and made a few gobbling sounds. She clucked, paused, and clucked again. The chill was just starting to creep into her when she detected sudden movement below. Her grip tightened on the shotgun as she aimed, peering down the scope.

The animal that appeared around the rocky ledge was not a turkey but a scruffy white coyote. Evelyn kept still; her station was elevated and upwind, out of the coyote's lines of sight and scent. The canine moved with a distinct limp as it sniffed around the scrubby pines, then squatted to mark a tree with scent. The coyote was female, then, and she'd had a nasty encounter with something that left her wounded.

The coyote vanished just as suddenly as she'd appeared, and Evelyn thought she must have given away her position until she glimpsed a grey-white tail slipping into a crevice among the rocks. When the coyote re-emerged, Evelyn got a good look at her through the scope. One of the coyote's eyes was cloudy and red-rimmed, and she was noticeably distressed. Soon she disappeared among the rocks once again. Evelyn watched as the coyote whined and paced in and out of the den at irregular intervals, even as the mist lifted and the sun rose.

Eventually, she switched the shotgun scope for her binoculars, and continued to watch for another half-hour as the coyote paced, whimpered, and occasionally defecated not far from the den.

It wasn't until Evelyn was already on her way back to the truck that it finally occurred to her—the coyote was not only injured, she was preparing to give birth.

➤

As had become her daily custom since moving her father into the home, Evelyn gave him a call in the early afternoon. She was relieved to find that he seemed to be having one of his good days.

"Hi dear, how's it going?" he said. "Bringing back a bird for your old man?"

"Trying, Dad, but I haven't seen much yet. How are you feeling?"

"Fine, fine," he said. "Food's decent here, I suppose, but nothing like your mother's cooking. Sure do miss the farm, you know."

"I miss it too," Evelyn said. "Especially this time of year, when everything's about to start growing."

"Louanne would be getting the garden ready just about now," he said. "She'd be out there all day, digging around and talking to the earth like it could speak right back to her."

Evelyn swallowed. She didn't have the heart to remind him that her mother's garden was long gone. In the few years between her mother's death and her father's deterioration, Evelyn had sold the farm to help pay for the old folks' home. A developer had already gone in and torn everything down, dividing the lot into what would become ten, maybe fifteen *New Luxury Countryside Homes.*

There was a lull in their talk, and her father began mumbling to himself.

"Can't wait to get back, eh. Spring's coming, I can smell it. This year I'm going to fix up the shed. Louanne's been on my case about it, and she's right. It's been falling apart for years."

Evelyn held the line, hoping that he would come back to himself.

"Dad—"

"That you, Louanne?"

"No, it's Evie."

"Eh?" he was practically shouting now. "Who?"

"Evie," she said as clearly and calmly as she could. "Evelyn. Your daughter."

"I'm expecting Louanne. She's supposed to be home soon."

"Okay, but maybe we can just talk for a bit—"

"I've got to keep the line open," he interrupted angrily. "In case Louanne calls. She might need a drive home. I've got to keep the line open."

"Dad—"

There was a click as he hung up. Evelyn stared at the screen of her cell. Beneath her boots the ground trembled as a quarry truck rumbled past. When it was well out of sight, she made her way through the woods and headed up the Mountain.

This time, she checked the wind and chose a new location that was closer to the den, only slightly lower, with a large spruce for cover. She set up her binoculars on a small tripod and focused on the rocky crevice as best she could. As the afternoon light shifted, she caught sight of white fur among the shadows. The coyote was lying on her side in the den, as though in repose, but she was restless—lifting a leg to lick at herself, shifting her weight, rearranging her paws, stretching her neck. When she closed her eyes, Evelyn could just barely make out the sound of heavy panting, and the occasional whine or moan.

The coyote shifted her position and Evelyn saw two small, writhing shapes that had already been cleaned of their fetal sacs. Something else glistened behind the mother's back legs, and Evelyn supressed a gasp as the coyote reached back, chewed off the umbilical cord with her teeth, and plucked the newborn up in her jaws. She set the pup between her front paws and began licking away the sac with slow, rhythmic patience. Evelyn thought she could even hear little high-pitched whines as the other pups suckled.

One by one, she witnessed the births of three more pups. The mother licked them clean, each pup receiving the same methodical care before being nudged into place among its siblings at her teats. All six had been born alive, and Evelyn knew from Maisy and the family's long-gone farm dogs that this wasn't always the case, even in easier circumstances. As the coyote emitted a final low, drawn-out howl, Evelyn was already imagining how she would describe the scene to her father. She wanted to laugh out loud, to lift her voice into a howl of her own and sing along with the mother coyote. She settled for grinning into her fist, clenched against the damp chill of early evening.

But a sense of foreboding crept over her as she watched the newborns blindly kneading and writhing against their mother, seeking to feed. The coyote's recent injuries were still healing, and Evelyn figured that giving birth had drained a lot of her energy. The coyote lay on her side, panting heavily. In regular circumstances, the male would bring food to the den as the mother nursed the litter—at least until the pups opened their eyes in a couple of weeks' time. But as far as she could tell, there was no male. Probably Nicholai had scraped his dead remains off the side of the quarry road, right where she'd left him.

Evelyn considered keeping vigil all night in the woods, wanting to be close to the wild mother and her newborns. To protect them and watch over them all until the morning. But when night closed in, she quickly packed up her gear and hurried away—sensing rather than seeing her way back through the trees.

➤

For the first night in weeks Evelyn slept all the way through till dawn. She filled a Thermos with fresh coffee and then rushed eagerly out the door. She pulled up to the usual spot and took a swig from the Thermos, then called her father on impulse. She knew she should stick to the regular schedule; the nurses were always going on about the importance of establishing routines for dementia patients. But her father was the only person she could imagine telling about the coyotes. After all, it was under his guidance on the farm that she'd grown familiar with the bloodier side of existence from a young age—birth and death seeping into one another through every life saved and every life taken, or lost.

Her father picked up on the second ring. "Morning, Evie," he said. "Everything all right?"

Evelyn was so relieved to hear his voice as it had always been, low and measured, that she leaned her head against the driver's side window and closed her eyes.

"Yes," she said. "Everything's fine. No turkeys yet, though."

"They're coming," he said. "Some years it's like that, eh. But they're coming."

"Hope so," she said. "Dad, I need your advice."

Evelyn told him about the coyotes—the first one dying on the roadside, and the second at the den on the Mountain—and recounted the birth. He listened closely, asking her to repeat certain details, saying it was a rare thing to have witnessed a birth in the wild.

"Imagine that, eh," he said. "I sure would've loved to be there."

"Me too, Dad." Evelyn took another sip of coffee. "The mother doesn't look too good, though. I'm not sure she'll make it."

There was a pause, and she braced herself for one of his sudden swings. But his voice was still steady when he spoke again.

"Evie, you know you should walk away and let nature do what it needs to do," he said.

"Yeah," she said, with a quaver in her voice. "I know."

"Coyotes aren't scarce, you know. They're the hardiest damn creatures in North America, and that's a known fact. They'll be around long after we're all just dust."

"I know," she repeated. "It's just—"

"It's never easy, making decisions about birth and death." He paused. "You know that, too."

Evelyn fiddled with the Thermos cap and took another sip, choking the bitter coffee down and wiping her mouth on the back

of her hand. She wanted to apologize to him for everything—
the failed turkey hunt, the injured coyote, selling the farm, the
unborn grandbabies, all of it.

"I'll call the Wildlife Services people in," she found herself
saying instead. "Just in case. Maybe there's a chance for her—and
for the pups, too."

"You've got good sense, Evie," he replied. "I know you'll do
what you need to do."

Evelyn sat unmoving in the driver's seat for a few minutes
after they hung up, staring at the long, empty road. Then she
drained the rest of the coffee, tossed the Thermos aside, and
got out. After pulling on her camo jacket, she leaned against the
tailgate and sent a quick reply to Sue about the baby shower: *I
can't make it today, but wishing you and the little one all the best.*
Then she looped the binoculars around her neck and trotted
into the woods.

Moving noiselessly through the spruce, Evelyn took a meandering route up the Mountain to the den. The wind was blowing
in a westerly way, which could alert the mother coyote to her
presence long before Evelyn even arrived. As she passed a rocky
outcrop, she heard agitated clucks and a mad ruffling of wings—
she had spooked a few turkeys from their roost. Bemused, she
stared after them as they scuttled away into the woods. She didn't
even have her shotgun on her this time.

Evelyn picked up her pace, binoculars swinging from her
neck. After she found the den again and settled into her hiding
spot, she paused with her eyes closed, listening. The surrounding
woods were alive with the sounds of melting and the first tentative voices of the season's early songbirds—robins and yellow
warblers. But she couldn't catch any noises coming from the den.
Looking through her binoculars into the cleft in the rock, Evelyn
could just make out the shape of the mother coyote lying stiffly
on her side. The lenses fogged over, and Evelyn let them dangle
from the neck strap.

She half crawled toward the den, stopping every metre or so to look first with the binoculars, then with her naked eyes as she approached the den. She waited in a crouch—was that mewling? The sound was so feeble that it seemed half-imagined. Finally, Evelyn leaned forward and peered into the dim hollow.

Closer examination confirmed what she had feared. The mother coyote was dead—but only recently, she thought, as she hovered her fingertips over the body and felt a faint, lingering warmth. The pups, curled in a heap by her teats, were too still. Up close, she could see that the coyote's injuries, including the blinded eye, had been the result of buckshot. *Jason takes a crack at them whenever he can.* A blue jay called a warning from a branch above. Evelyn sank back into a heavy squat.

A sudden squirm among the litter. The faintest of squeaks. Two of the pups, one silver-white and the other dark grey, were still struggling to stay alive. Eyes sealed, they prodded feebly at their mother's body, hungry, begging to be fed.

"There you are," she murmured, inching closer. "Look at you."

Evelyn knew she should leave the pups for other scavengers needing to feed their own young. It was like her father said—coyotes weren't rare. Countless others would be born that season, season after season, and the cycle would go on with or without her intervention. It was the way of wild things. But her hands found the two live pups of their own volition. She breathed in the scent of birth and milk, fur and earth.

Evelyn settled back, her lap full of whimpering fuzz. Tightening the space made by her crossed legs, she tried to warm them; she could feel their living heat radiating through her inner thighs. Evelyn ran a finger over the little sealed eyes. Then the sudden sharp echo of a gunshot reminded her that there were hunters in the woods.

She pulled off her toque with a crackle of static and swaddled the pups together in the thick wool. One of them emitted a small cry, and she stroked the soft space between its ears. The tiny, seeking mouths suckled at her thumbs. If she wasn't going to let nature run its course, then she should call Nicholai as soon as possible, so that the pups could receive the expert care they needed. There were guidelines for this kind of situation, she knew, and protocols to follow.

Another shot rang out. Evelyn tucked the mewling bundle into the front of her jacket, where the pups writhed against her chest. She moved further up the Mountain, making her way over the rocky ridge on all fours. Then she stood, reorienting herself to her surroundings.

Predators

Heidi checked her phone. No messages, and one new email from the university's Association for New Alumni—already asking for a donation. She trashed it, then shoved the phone into her back pocket. She still had a few minutes before she had to return inside for the rest of her shift at the pub, though she and old Jim Rizzo were keeping an honour system going for the hours she was picking up at Good Folks. She wasn't planning to stay in town for long, so she hadn't officially signed on to payroll.

She lit a cigarette and watched as a sleek black Tesla pulled into the parking lot. People in and around Sadowa mostly drove old vans and oversized pickups, but that wasn't the only reason why the car obviously belonged to an out-of-towner. It was the exacting way in which the driver, invisible behind the deeply-tinted side windows, parked the car between the faded yellow lines. Nobody local cared about those lines. With a smoky sigh, Heidi walked around to the back of the pub without waiting to get a glimpse of the driver.

A chain-link fence bordered the lot behind Good Folks, half-heartedly holding back two hundred acres of mixed-wood forest. A large sign riddled with pellet gun holes dangled at an angle from one of the posts. Notice of Public Meeting, it stated in bold black lettering, Concerning Application for Rezoning & Plan of Subdivision. Heidi didn't examine the fine print underneath—the sign had been put up a couple of months back, around the time she returned to Sadowa after graduating from university. She leaned against her white Toyota Tacoma and finished the cigarette, listening to the fluting song of a hermit thrush somewhere among the trees.

She noticed a coil of animal scat by the rear tire of her truck. Squatting for a closer look, she noted tawny animal fur and bone fragments. Heidi scanned the surrounding concrete, spotting a paw print in the muck of a nearby pothole. By its size, her first thought was *wolf*. But the pack that once lived in the area was long gone, so she settled on *coyote* instead. She tossed her cigarette aside and eyed the shape and width of the pads, then spotted a second track farther away. There was an opening in the fence by the sign where the wire had come unhooked and the fence was all bent out of shape. She walked over and fingered a snagged tuft of grey-white fur.

The back of her neck prickled. Heidi scanned the under-brush beyond the fence—was she being watched? How close wildness was, reaching over fences and pushing up through asphalt that was constantly cracking and splitting, giving way to the relentless weeds and roots. Coyotes, in particular, were circling closer. Earlier that week, Good Folks had hosted a town hall meeting about the recent uptick in coyote encounters.

As she rubbed the fur between her thumb and forefinger, the pub's back door squeaked open and Jim Rizzo appeared on the threshold.

"Mr. Big Shot's just come in—wants whiskey on the rocks. Go ask if he'll have the daily special with that, will you?"

"Got it."

Heidi released the tuft of fur into the wind. Although she hadn't said anything during the coyote discussion at the meeting, she figured she knew more than the average Sadowan. She'd taken first-year ecology at college, where she'd learned that effective coyote management meant balancing out the entire food chain. In other words, if the townsfolk really wanted to get rid of the coyotes, then technically they should bring back the wolves.

Retying her red apron around her waist, Heidi followed her boss back into the dingy pub. She took the drink Jim already prepared at the bar and made her way to the dingy corner where the Tesla driver was seated, typing on his phone. He was the only customer. His earbuds glowed blue in the gloom. Above him hung a crooked whiteboard from the town hall meeting, on which the word COYOTES was scrawled.

"Sorry for the wait," Heidi said.

"No problem," he said, slightly too loudly, without looking up.

"Can I interest you in the daily special?" she asked, setting the drink down before him. "Burger combo. Extra fries."

Her voice came out high pitched, sounding girlish and uncertain. He popped out one of his earbuds.

"Sorry, what's that?" he asked. After she repeated herself about the special, he said: "Sure thing."

Back in the kitchen, Heidi confirmed the order with Jim. They exchanged a knowing glance. The Tesla driver wasn't entirely a stranger, after all. His name was Alonzo Jones, and he represented a big development firm from the city. After the coyote deregulation debate at the meeting, he'd given a presentation about land development in Sadowa. He'd started off with a joke: "Well, if you want to get rid of your coyote problem, why not claim their habitat as your own?" Nobody laughed.

He'd gone on to outline the new subdivision his firm was planning to build in Sadowa, featuring sixty-three residential units, a shopping plaza, a small kids' park and a smaller, fenced, off-leash area for dogs. He projected a slideshow from his MacBook: graphs, budget estimates, and aerial photographs of town boundaries, forested land, and property lines. Sadowa would even get a connection along the commuter bus line into the city, and the town could be rebranded as "Countryside Close to the City." All that was needed for this shiny new future was for the two hundred acres of forested land behind Good Folks to be rezoned for recreational and commercial development.

Heidi had noticed the townsfolk shifting in their seats and giving one another skeptical looks—they hadn't considered Sadowa and its surroundings as a product to be marketed. She herself had just spent four years in the city, so she figured she had a better understanding of how things worked. Anyway, Alonzo Jones certainly seemed to know what he was talking about.

When Heidi returned to his table with his order, Jones looked at her almost familiarly—as though trying to place her. This time, she held his gaze.

"You were here during the meeting, weren't you?" he asked, taking out one of his earbuds again.

"The town hall? Yeah."

Jones unfolded a napkin and spread it over his lap. "So what do you think of the proposal, then?"

She was startled to be asked such a direct question. She recalled from his talk that his firm had already bought a twenty-acre farm at the edge of town, and were in the process of developing a community of luxury country homes. During his presentation, Jones had explained that the new project would be even grander in scale, which would trigger a population boom and a considerable boost to the local economy.

"I guess it will be good for the local economy," Heidi said.

He gave her a smile. "Smart girl."

She flushed, feeling stupidly pleased. She wanted to tell him that she had just finished her degree and was planning on applying to grad school—just as soon as she made up her mind. But Jones had already put his earbud back in, and was typing busily on his phone again.

The bell clanked above the tavern door as Heidi made her way through the rows of empty tables to the bar. The newcomer seated himself on a barstool, and Heidi drew back when she recognized Nate Malone. The last time she'd seen him was when she'd broken up with him—had she actually said that she was going places and he wasn't?

"Hey, Heidi," he said with a big smile. "Heard you were back. Wanted to see for myself."

Nate had broad shoulders now, and a neatly trimmed beard, beneath which his smile was as disarming as ever. Heidi brought him the coke he requested, and they exchanged polite updates about their lives. When she'd left, Nate had been jobless and his main interests were drinking beer and shooting at empty cans with a .22 in his backyard. Now he was working for the Northern Emergency Services, assisting with forest fire evacuations in remote communities. It had been four years—they had both grown up and moved on.

Nate listened intently as Heidi leaned against the bar and outlined her options for the near future: law school, a master's degree, an internship, or going abroad. She felt her face getting hot as she prattled on. Never mind that she was back in Sadowa at her old job, as though she'd never left town in the first place.

"Always knew great things were coming," Nate said, raising his coke in her direction.

She offered to bring him a Moosehead Lager, remembering that it had been his favourite beer. But he declined, saying that he no longer drank.

"It was the EMS training—got me all cleaned up. Even quit smoking."

"That's great," she said, her voice cracking slightly. She'd started smoking again since returning to Sadowa. She wondered if he could smell it on her.

The tavern started filling up with the dinner crowd, and Heidi hurried off to serve them. Classic rock jangled in the background as the murky interior filled with shouted greetings and jokey conversation among friends. Most of the clientele were familiar old-timers. One of Nate's uncles came in—the one who wore camo for all occasions—and started talking about survivalism with his nephew. The uncle was well known for his belief in the crumbling world order and the importance of being relentlessly self-reliant.

Eavesdropping as she manoeuvred trays of food and beer among the tables, Heidi learned that Nate had recently bought a plot of land adjacent to the forested lot behind Good Folks. He had already built an insulated cabin and was slowly setting up his own survivalist camp. The uncle's place, everyone knew, was located deep in the woods north of Sadowa, where it was rumoured that he bred coydogs for added protection.

"Hey, now," Nate said, when the older man said he hadn't paid taxes since he was Nate's age. "You know those tax dollars go towards firefighting and search-and-rescue operations—so basically me and my job, eh?"

"Well, then," his uncle replied, his voice booming across the room, "if I ever go missing in the bush, kid, you can just leave me out there to rot."

"Right on," Nate replied, laughing. "Can I get that in writing?"

"You can get it in blood!" his uncle bellowed, and they clinked glasses as the other men around them guffawed.

Heidi kept herself busy with orders, embarrassed by their outlaw mentality. She wondered what Jones was thinking—how he must see the town and its people, as his company planned the future of Sadowa from a distance; redrawing the map, deciding the potential and most efficient use of the surrounding land. *I don't belong here,* she wanted to say. *I'm not one of them. I went to college. I know more than you think.*

But Jones was riveted to his phone, seeming hardly aware that the pub was filling up around him. When he finally asked Heidi for the bill, she saw that he'd hardly touched the burger and fries. She was making her way back to the kitchen with his plate, eyeing the soggy fries, when Nate's uncle's voice boomed out again.

"You'd better watch yourself around here, eh."

The pub fell silent as Jones, halfway between his table and the door, calmly removed an earbud.

"Huh, what was that?" he asked, smiling blandly at the burly, red-faced man blocking his exit.

"I said watch yourself," the uncle dropped his voice to a low rumble. "We don't want your fancy plans around here."

Jones just kept smiling and looking up at him, as though expecting the older man to continue with an explanation. Heidi retreated behind the bar, kept her head down as she wiped up around the draft taps.

"You hear me, kid?"

"Yes, sir, I hear you," Jones said. He spoke slowly. "I'll be sure to keep that in mind."

The uncle stepped aside, and Alonzo Jones left the pub without a backward glance. Within moments, Good Folks was humming with conversation again. Heidi went to clear the corner table and found an unexceptional tip next to the crumpled napkin. Deflated, she watched through the greasy window as the Tesla made a precise three-point turn, exited the parking lot, and disappeared down the regional road. Heidi wiped down the table until it was spotless, and then moved on to the next.

It was almost midnight when Jim told her that she was free to leave, saying he could handle the rest of the night on his own. Heidi tallied a few more bills, tugged off her apron, grabbed her jacket, and was about to slip out the door when she felt a light touch on her arm. Nate's face swam into view.

"Hey, need a drive home?"

Why didn't she just tell him that her own truck was parked out back? Her parents' place was close enough that she could have walked, if it wasn't so bloody dark out. Instead, she found herself following Nate out to his grey Ford Ranger, which shone silver under the rising half moon. The truck was new. Back when they were dating he'd been driving a beat-up black pickup of his father's.

As they headed north along the road, Heidi reached out to stroke the coarse white fur of a coyote tail dangling from the rear-view mirror. Nate was filling her in about some of their high school acquaintances. There had been a few unlikely marriages, several babies, a divorce, a disappearance, a suicide.

Sitting this close to Nate in the confines of the truck, she could smell woodsmoke on him. It was oddly comforting after all this time. She recalled her parents' relief when she told them about the breakup. They'd been worried that she might end up staying in Sadowa with him, instead of accepting one of her college offers. But they didn't realize that she hadn't thought twice about the decision. She had never even considered staying.

During a lull in their small talk, Heidi asked what he thought of the scene his uncle made at the pub.

"Yeah, he gets a bit riled up. But I can't blame him, really. I'm getting sick of these developers myself—prowling around, acting like they own the place."

"Alonzo Jones asked me my opinion about the proposal," she said. "Guess he's trying to get an idea of what the residents are thinking."

He shot her a glance, and she immediately regretted her use of the word *residents*.

"Yeah, no doubt," he said. "There's a lot of resistance. What did you tell him?"

"Oh, just that I'd have to see more research. You know, to get a sense of the bigger picture."

She wished she'd said something along those lines, instead of parroting the guy's own words back at him.

Nate scoffed. "Come on, it's a terrible proposal," he said. "His company is buying up all the land around Sadowa, outbidding anyone local, making decisions about what the town's going to look like in a few years' time. It's bullshit."

"Yeah, sure," she said. She was dying for a cigarette. "But I guess it'll be good for the local economy."

"Good for the economy, or good for us? Nobody currently living in Sadowa could afford to buy one of these fancy mansions. We're getting pushed out."

Heidi gazed out the passenger-side window. She hadn't considered that. She'd grown up in a modular home on a lot that backed onto the forest's edge, where she used to build tree forts and set up maple-tapping buckets in the woods. The houses pictured in the promotional brochures were dream homes, certainly, but they were dreams that somebody had conjured up a long way from Sadowa.

Just as Heidi opened her mouth to say that she agreed with him, something white and shaggy materialized on the road ahead; she cried out, and Nate somehow managed to slow the truck to a stop without swerving or jamming down on the brakes. As the animal darted away, lean and ghost pale, Heidi drew a shaky breath. A pair of eyes gleamed briefly from the dark mass of the woods before disappearing with a blink.

"All good," Nate said, giving her knee a light squeeze. "You okay?"

"Just spooked." She tried to laugh off her nerves. "It's true about the coyotes, eh? They really are taking over."

"Not coyotes." He eased the truck into drive again. "Coywolves."

"You mean like your uncle's coydogs?"

He kept his eyes on the road and didn't answer. His uncle's breeding efforts were probably illegal.

After a moment he said: "Did you see the size of that one? No way it's just a coyote."

It sounded like some kind of Sasquatch theory. But there had been something about the canine's face—the snout was long, wolfish. Heidi recalled the oversized paw print in the Good Folks' parking lot, and the bygone wolf pack that older Sadowans talked about. Was it possible that the wolves hadn't retreated to remote northern regions, after all? Instead, they could have mated with coyotes migrating from urban areas in the south, the two predators hybridizing over time until they emerged as something in between.

"So all this is mine," Nate was saying, gesturing at the mass of spruces lining the right-hand side of the road. "Way back in there is the cabin and everything."

Nate explained how lucky he'd been that the previous owner agreed to a private sale, before the developers could pounce on the land. He clicked the high beams to low and back to high again as they passed another vehicle. Heidi was scanning the gravel shoulder as they swept along, still looking for signs that there was a new predator in the woods.

"You know, I'd love to see the new place," she said, after a pause. "Since we're already here."

His eyes flicked from the road to her face and back again.

"Sure," he said. "But it's a work-in-progress, really. Not quite ready yet."

They were quiet until the next bend in the road. Nate eased the truck through a gap in the trees that was only discernible from the surrounding bush by a reflective NO TRESPASSING sign nailed to a stump.

"Here we are, then," he said.

The driveway was long and meandering. The trees gradually thinned out into a clearing, where Nate brought the truck to stop in front of a small cabin. The metal roof glinted in the moonlight. They got out, and a series of motion-activated lights came on as Nate gave Heidi a brief tour of the refuge he was readying for the end of the world. Amenities included a composting toilet and woodstove, generators, water purifiers, medical supplies, a greenhouse, and well-stocked outbuildings. Nate's survivalist camp wasn't yet complete, but it was already impressively self-sufficient.

As she listened to him describing the new storehouse he was planning to build next, it occurred to Heidi that he was preparing for a very different future than the one she was trying to figure out. He was envisioning a world that was almost apocalyptic, in which most of her current preoccupations wouldn't matter—a future she hadn't even considered. She wondered if they would be working on the camp together, if she hadn't left.

"Wow," she said, gazing around. "Seems like a lot of effort."

"It's just a hobby, really," he said. "I'm not obsessed like some preppers are—people go a little crazy, stockpiling weapons and building an underground compound, or whatever. I just like the idea of being prepared."

A bark sounded somewhere in the woods. More wild voices joined in with a series of yips, blending together and then pulling apart again into a sequence of distinct barks that sounded almost like laughter. Then they gathered into a single, drawn-out howl.

"Coywolves," Heidi said, saying the word aloud for the first time. "It's them, isn't it?"

"Yeah."

They stood side-by-side, listening to the wild chorus for a little while longer. A final howl severed the hushed space between them—sounding closer than the others.

"Maybe we should go inside," Nate said, his voice so low she had to lean closer to hear him.

Heidi hesitated only briefly, shivering in the evening breeze, then nodded and followed him into the cabin. They exchanged only a few words as he gathered kindling and a few logs and got a fire going in the woodstove. Even with the flames flickering behind the grate, it was so dark in the one-room space that she could barely discern the shape of his body from the shadows. He could be anyone, really, as he reached for her.

>

Heidi woke well before dawn. She lay listening to the hiss of the dying fire. She sensed Nate's animal warmth next to her, but he didn't stir. How simple it would be, to settle back into her old life here. But at the same time, how easy it could be to drift away again. She couldn't shake the feeling she'd had since graduating and returning to Sadowa to figure things out—the feeling that she no longer belonged anywhere in particular.

Anxiety overtook her slowly, like something crawling all over her skin.

She sat up, gasping. Nate shifted in his sleep, but didn't waken. Heidi groped around for her clothes, and pulled them on as quietly as she could. She sat on the edge of the bed, tracing the shadowy trail through her surroundings in her mind: past the glowing embers in the stove, through the cabin door, down the steps and along the winding driveway from Nate's place; then following the road around the forest to the parking lot behind Good Folks, to her truck. She could be home in less than an hour.

Briefly, Heidi wondered what Nate would think if she just left. *Again*, she reminded herself—if she left all over again. She considered the tender way he had removed her clothes, the sweet words he'd whispered into her hair afterward. But she had already made up her mind. She stood and made her way, barefoot, to the door.

Out on the porch Heidi yanked on her shoes. She hesitated on the steps, reminding herself that she knew these woods, these country roads. It was, in a sense, her natural habitat. She zipped her jacket up to her chin and headed down the driveway. When she was out of sight of the cabin, she slowed her pace and listened. The coyotes—or coywolves, or whoever they were—were silent.

At the end of the driveway, she paused and looked up and down the unlit road. Shoving her hands deep into her jacket pockets, she walked in the direction of the town. She half expected to hear Nate calling for her to come back. The density of the woods pressed toward her from both gravel shoulders—on one side was Nate's property, and on the other was the forest that also bordered the Good Folks parking lot.

She was reaching into her jacket pocket for a cigarette when something darted across her path. She fumbled with her phone and tapped its flashlight on—it was just a rabbit she had spooked from the shadows.

She switched the light off, but the rabbit remained starkly outlined on the road before her. Heidi's heart was pounding, and her whole body was tensed up. A vehicle was coming in her direction, high beams searing through the night. She hopped over the waterlogged pocket of the ditch before ducking into a stand of spruce at the forest's edge. The vehicle slowed as it approached, and Heidi recognized the Tesla as the rabbit finally bolted off the road and bounded right past her, retreating into the bush.

The Tesla came to a full stop, and after a few moments Alonzo Jones got out. Heidi shrank back; he must have seen her out on the road. How could she explain why she was wandering around in the middle of nowhere at night, lurking in the bush like she had something to hide? She braced herself, expecting him to call out or to laugh in her direction. But soon she realized that Jones wasn't aware of her presence. At first she thought he was talking to himself. Then she glimpsed the blue glow of his earbuds as he started manoeuvring a large, flat object out of the backseat of the car.

"Listen," he was saying. "If I put the sign up, the locals might assume that it's already a done deal. Meaning there'll be less public pushback to deal with, so we can focus on the administrative side and get this one done and over with."

There was a pause as he extracted the object out of the backseat.

"Yeah, I know. But if we don't snag this project—and soon—someone else will. It's only a matter of time."

In the pool of light spilling from the Tesla's open doors, Heidi watched as Jones turned from the car and headed in her direction with what appeared to be an enormous rectangle of cardboard. There was a splashing sound as he staggered through the ditch.

"Fucking Christ," he yelped. "No—nothing," he said after a pause, his voice taking on an impatient edge. "Just trust me, okay? It's a strategy that worked with the last project. Let's keep up the momentum." Another pause. "Yeah, okay. Talk soon."

He started tearing branches off a nearby sapling just a few metres away from Heidi's hiding spot. She cowered, keeping her gaze lowered, thinking for an irrational second that her eyes might shine in the dark like an animal's. Four hammer strikes rang out in swift succession; Heidi cringed as they reverberated through the roots underfoot. Then Jones sloshed back through the ditch, muttering to himself. He tossed the hammer into the backseat and went around to the driver's side. The back door appeared to slide shut of its own accord and soon the Tesla slipped beyond her range of sight, gliding away without a sound.

Scrambling back onto the road, Heidi stood on the gravel shoulder and looked up at the large sign the jerk had nailed to the tree. It glowed a phosphorescent white in the moonlight—there was no need to use her phone's flashlight for a closer look. The sign was emblazoned with the logo of Jones' company, beneath which it read: Development Land Coming Soon! Followed by: Supporting the Growth of Our Communities. There was an oversized photo of a little girl in a pink dress smiling on a swing, with a tidy row of redbrick townhomes in the background.

As Heidi looked up at the sign, the forest slowly transformed into a suburb before her—complete with houses, lawns, driveways, and streetlights. The little girl was laughing—kicking her legs as she swung back and forth—and the redbrick houses marched on and on, reaching into the distance, into the future.

A breeze rattled the bare branches of a nearby silver birch, which stood out, ghost like, from the surrounding spruce. The breeze died down and the forest took on a braced stillness, as though waiting to see what Heidi would do next.

She hesitated. Tomorrow, at work, she could tell somebody about what Alonzo Jones had said; she could recount the conversation she'd overheard, and the townsfolk would rally together and run the land developers out of Sadowa for good. But she didn't want to wait until somebody else figured it out. Instead, Heidi surged forward and clawed at the sign, tugging and tearing at the cardboard until she'd managed to rip most of it down.

When she was done, Heidi kicked the shreds into the ditch. Then she sagged against a tree. She still had a forty-minute walk ahead of her. The fastest way back would be to take a shortcut through part of the forest, to the Good Folks parking lot just on the other side. It wasn't too far. The moon had faded behind wispy clouds, but it would be sunrise soon enough. Heidi took a small step forward, arms outstretched, and started pushing her way through the trees.

A twig snapped nearby and she held still. Loud yips sounded in the distance. An alert silence followed, until a bark rang out—closer this time—followed by a strangled noise, a whimper in the dark. Heidi sprang forward, holding up her arms to protect her face from the underbrush as she stumbled over roots and fallen branches. Something shifted in the woods to her right—no, right in front of her, or maybe just behind. She became aware of a shuffling sound nearby.

Heidi tripped and pitched forward, landing hard on her palms in the dirt. She staggered up and went crashing through the underbrush until she glimpsed a distant light through the trees. It was the bare bulb above the back door of the pub—wasn't it? A few more strides and she'd be at the fence. She'd scale the rickety chain-link, or else crawl through the gap on her hands and knees. There was a metallic taste in her mouth. She was breathless and wheezing. She kept on running. She was almost there.

Johnny Blue

She's driving too fast again, trying to stretch the distance between us and the mess we've left behind. Beside me, Johnny Blue is bashing around in his birdcage. I'm worried he might damage his wings.

"Ma!" My voice comes out hoarse. "Slow down. Look, it's the next exit."

My mother wipes at her sweaty forehead with a fist. She eases the pickup truck along the off-ramp, passing the sign that says Welcome to Washago. It's a relief to finally get off the wide, multi-lane highway—it was too open, too exposed. Anybody could've been following us.

Ma lights a cigarette. I open my window a crack and let in a cool blast of spring air along with the roar of the nearby Severn River. Then I poke my finger through the bars of the cage, stroking Johnny Blue's beak. He gives me a playful nip in return.

"Shit," Ma says, her voice panicky. "Oh, Jesus."

The ramp is flooded—entirely washed out, swallowed up by the swollen Severn River. But what's worse is the police cruiser nearby, positioned on higher ground with its lights flashing. The officers are wearing chest waders, flagging down cars, redirecting traffic, talking to drivers. They've set up a bunch of orange pylons, and half of them are already floating away. We exchange a glance over the birdcage, and I push the button to close the window again.

Problem is, the truck we're driving is stolen. Technically, it belongs to Ma's boyfriend. Ex-boyfriend, I guess, now that we've packed up and left. This time, she says we won't be going back. We've been driving all night, straight through the grey dawn. We took the truck because the money he used to pay for it—at least part of it was Ma's. Could've paid off the credit cards, could've paid off everybody we've taken or borrowed from. But instead he went out and bought himself a Dodge Ram 1500, in flame red.

An officer waves us forward, and suddenly it's like someone sucked all the oxygen out of the truck. Johnny Blue makes a garbled sound, turning in awkward half circles on his perch.

The other problem is that Ma doesn't have a driver's license. Not anymore, at least. It got suspended a few weeks back, even though she says she didn't have all that much to drink that night. Her hands look like claws, so tight on the wheel that I can see her knucklebones poking through the skin. Other than Johnny Blue rustling his wings, the only sound is the clicking of the windshield wipers going back and forth.

But the officer signals for Ma to keep driving past the pylons, since the pickup is big enough to move safely through the water. Other cars get pulled over and have to turn back. Ma taps the hazard lights on and noses us into the flood, water spraying out from both sides of the truck. Soon enough, the cops are out of sight and I can breathe again. Johnny Blue finally quits pacing, and clings to his perch.

We don't say another word until we reach a stop sign sticking crookedly up from the brown water. Ma sucks hard on her cigarette.

"We'll get through this, kiddo," she says. "Like we always do. Just me and you."

"And Johnny Blue," I add.

"Me and you and Johnny Blue," she repeats, releasing a mouthful of smoke. The way she says it sounds almost like a song.

The water becomes shallower as we drive on, until it's mostly just puddles and greasy clay. Ma switches off the hazard lights, but she's still using the all-wheel drive. The last time we visited Washago, which is where she grew up, Ma taught me how to drive along these dirt roads—bouncing over potholes and churning up gravel. She called me a natural behind the wheel, even though I was just barely thirteen. The flooding's gotten worse since then. Three waterways pass through the town—the wide Severn, and the narrower and deeper Black and Muddy Rivers. It doesn't even have to rain; the rivers seem to flood whenever they feel like it— sometimes just one, sometimes all three at once. Residents often take canoes or paddleboats to the grocery store instead of cars. Kids wear life jackets walking to school, just in case.

We pass a white chapel on a hill with a sign out front that says: Jesus Loves Virgins! It's nice to hear Ma laugh. She lowers the window and flicks away the cigarette butt, letting in a waft of a rotten-egg smell—the stink of foul standing water.

When we arrive at the Welcome Home Motel, located across the Severn from the white chapel, half the parking lot is flooded. Ma gets us a room, then parks the truck around back where it can't be seen from the road. She carries her suitcase over her head as we slosh through ankle-deep, shit-brown water to the door. I've got my backpack on and I'm carrying Johnny Blue in his cage, which I set down on the little round table by the window. A single bed is pressed against the wood-paneled wall. An old regional map hangs over the nightstand, slightly crooked in a cracked glass frame.

Ma kicks off her shoes and picks up a brochure by the phone, as she sits on the edge of the bed. She reads aloud: "Plan your summer getaway in Washago—where three rivers meet!" She snorts and holds it up to show me a photo of a fancy yacht on the front. "Would you look at that! Maybe we can do a little sightseeing."

Even I have to laugh a little. Sometimes seasonal cottagers pass through Washago on their yachts, following the Severn from Lake Couchiching to Georgian Bay, or vice versa. Ma always says the flooding problems started when they did something at the mouth of the river, expanding the riverbank with fill so that more cottages could be built along the waterfront. The rivers were half choked, and nothing was the same after that.

"So here's the plan," Ma says, tossing the brochure aside. "We'll sell the truck for cash. We can buy a small car instead, nothing special, and still have plenty of money left over. After that, we can go wherever we want."

Johnny Blue rattles at the bars of his cage with his talons, ruffling his grey feathers. I sprinkle birdseed and grits at the bottom of his cage and he starts pecking away, tilting his head every so often to peer at me through the bars. He's just a pigeon, basically a rat of a bird, but he's got the bluest eyes I've ever seen.

"Okay," I say at last, stroking Johnny Blue's feathers with a fingertip.

I figure Ma will ask Aunt Caro if we can crash at her place for a bit, just until we get back on our feet—like we did last time. The time before that, we stayed with Grandma. Ma picks up the beige phone on the nightstand and dials.

I sit down beside her on the edge of the bed. "Aunt Caro?" I ask in a whisper.

She shakes her head. "Trying Grandma first."

Ma's quiet for a long time, with the phone pressed to her ear. Her expression is unreadable, and I guess the phone just keeps on ringing. Picking up the brochure, I start reading about the history of the Severn River. From the mid-nineteenth century up until 1920, the Severn was used to transport logs to sawmills located downriver. There's a black-and-white photo of some bearded white men standing around a pile of logs, with a sawmill looming in the background. Taking a closer look, I think I recognize the mill—now abandoned and sagging into the Severn somewhere between Washago and the next town.

Ma hangs up the phone with an impatient click of her tongue. I'm reading about how the Severn River used to be called *Matchetache*. The brochure doesn't explain why the name was changed, or when. Ma is dialing again.

Secretly, I'm relieved when she sighs and hangs up the second time. I don't really want to see Grandma again. Last time we were in town, staying with some cousins at her trailer, I stole a tin of cookies. Grandma interrogated each cousin separately, then all of us together, thinking we were all in on the theft. We had to place our hands on her Bible and swear in God's name that we didn't know what happened to the cookies. I was pretty proud of myself for keeping a straight face the entire time. The other cousins cried.

The next day, finding the empty tin under my mattress, Grandma was red faced with fury. She turned and told Ma she knew exactly what I was, and who I took after.

"Caro it is, then," Ma says, picking up the phone again.

I put the brochure aside and unlatch the door to the birdcage. Johnny Blue hops out, onto my finger, stretching his wings as he sidesteps along my arm. He perches on my shoulder, just like I trained him. He coos in my ear, and I get a whiff of his woodchip smell—a little musty, but also earthy and a bit sweet. I found him when he was still a fledgling, just learning how to fly.

Suddenly Ma sits up straight, and runs her fingers through her fake-red hair.

"Hi Caro," she says into the phone. "It's me. I'm in town." There's a long pause, and her expression darkens as she says: "What? You're kidding me. Why didn't you tell—wait, Caro, don't just—"

She's glassy eyed as she lowers the phone—is she angry or sad, or something else? For a few moments, the only sound is Johnny Blue making his little tutting noises as he preens his feathers.

Eventually, I clear my throat and announce in a teacherly voice: "Did you know the Severn used to be called River Matchetache?"

Ma is staring out the window. Dark blue clouds are piling up on the horizon. I get up and take a hand towel from the bathroom, which smells like the toilet's been backing up lately. I toss the towel over my shoulder and get Johnny Blue settled again on the frayed, off-white fabric. I've learned the hard way that you can't be too careful. Johnny Blue shits where he wants.

"I have to go out for a bit," Ma says as she gets up and grabs her purse from the bed. "You stay here, you hear me? Look, you can watch TV."

She thumbs a few buttons on the remote until she lands on a channel playing little-kid cartoons. Ma tugs on her wet sneakers. They squeak as she walks to the door.

"But Ma, where are you going?"

"You stay here," she repeats. "I'll be right back."

Then she's gone, taking the only key with her. Over the TV, I can hear the truck rumble to life before splashing away. Sitting cross-legged on the bed, I flip through the channels, which are mostly just static over and over again, until I come across a guy wearing a white suit and holding a microphone. His fingers gleam with fat gold rings.

"*Seek* in the Lord, for *he* is seeking *you!*" He looks kind of crazy. "Hold your hand to your TV screen, folks." He closes his eyes and raises his fist. "Yes! I *feel* your presence! The *Lord* is present, too. He's here, waiting for you. So call the toll-free number at the bottom of your screen, and make a donation now."

I have nothing better to do, so I pick up the phone and dial the number. I can't really say whether I'm expecting angels, the preacher, maybe even God Himself. But the line just rings and rings. What a joke. I hang up and switch the TV off, thinking I should know better, anyway. You can't ask for help too many times.

I wipe out the mess at the bottom of the birdcage, get Johnny Blue settled back in, and give him more grits. As he pecks away, I take a closer look at the historical map on the wall. The descriptive crest in the top corner says it was drawn by a surveyor in 1793. There's a long, winding river labelled *Matchetache*—so it's actually a map of right here, where I am. But there's no sign of Black or Muddy Rivers, and the areas to the north and west have been left empty, labelled "Great Tract of Woodland," and a little further up, "Indian Hunting Country" and "Immense Forest." Looks like it was drawn by somebody who'd never actually been here.

The phone rings and I jump—the map comes crashing down and Johnny Blue lets out a squawk. I reach for the receiver, then hesitate. Maybe it's my mother. It could also be Aunt Caro, or maybe Grandma, calling us back. Or the preacher, calling for my donation. Fourth ring, fifth. I think of Ma's boyfriend, even the police. Finally, I pick up and all I hear is a few seconds of crackling silence, then the drone of a dial tone.

My hands are shaking as I hang up. I shove the map and its splintered frame under the bed, then crawl under the damp, moldy-smelling blanket and pull it up to my chin. I close my eyes, imagining what the map would look like now, if somebody soared above Washago like a bird and looked down—three swollen rivers merging into one big, swampy mess, roadways leading right into the rising water and disappearing without a trace. Houses drifting along until they finally come to rest on dry land, somewhere far away.

➤

I wake up hungry. Johnny Blue's still sleeping, his head tucked under his wing. After putting on my cold, soaked runners, I fold the brochure between the bolt and the latch so the door can't automatically lock me out. I half walk, half wade down the road to the nearby gas station. I don't have any money on me, so I hang around the *Archie* comics until another customer arrives. He's buying some batteries and two 24-packs of bottled water.

"Hey Rick, stocking up?"

"You betcha. You got the evacuation call, eh?"

"Sure did, just a few minutes ago. You aren't leaving, either?"

"Nah. Not yet, at least. We're okay where we are, you know, up on the hill."

"Sure. They're calling for more rain tonight, eh, so just make sure you don't end up like what's-her-name from the trailer park."

The cashier shakes his head sadly.

As they keep talking, I manage to slip out of the store with a can of cream soda and a package of nuts shoved up my sleeve. Easy.

Back at the motel, I grab Johnny Blue's cage before heading out again. This time, I walk down to the swollen banks of the slow-moving river. I set the cage next to me on a bench overlooking the water, then remove my soaking socks and runners. The grass is soggy and I feel the chill seeping into my bare feet right away. I offer a few nuts to Johnny Blue before devouring the rest myself and washing down the salty mix with cream soda.

Across the river, a funeral is taking place at the white chapel on the hill. Teeny-tiny people dressed in black move as a single mass down the church steps and into the surrounding cemetery grounds, where dozens of teeny-tiny gravestones poke up from the grass.

Beside me, Johnny Blue keeps opening and refolding his wings, edging back and forth on his perch.

"Hey buddy, come on, it's okay."

Thunder rumbles in the distance and he flaps nervously, his wings hitting the bars. A bunch of ducks floats by, muttering among themselves. A robin belts out its evening song from a nearby bush, and Johnny Blue lets out a little squawk. He was so small and ugly when I found him, his beak and feet too big for his body. But he'd peered up at me from the sewer grate where he'd gotten caught up in some plastic bottles and candy wrappers, and I couldn't help myself. Since then he's come with us to and from Washago, and to whatever place we happen to be calling home. He knows everything.

When he squawks again, I unlatch the cage door and let it swing open. He pokes his head out and then steps onto my finger, talons lightly pinching at my skin. When he hops up to my shoulder, I catch the woodsy smell of him just before he spreads his wings and lifts away. In a few seconds I lose sight of him among the trees.

I latch the door again and sit there swinging my legs. Across the river, the funeral is over. The people dressed in black are already gone, and now there's just a teeny-tiny tractor filling in the hole they left behind. Thunder rolls closer, and it starts spitting rain. When I stand up, the water's already up to my ankles. Carrying my shoes in one hand and Johnny Blue's cage in the other, I make my way back to the motel and let myself into the room.

For a long time, I just sit on the bed with the empty cage in my lap.

>

Ma's in a bad mood when she finally gets back—it's late, after dark, and the rain is tapping against the window. She flops down on the bed and lights a cigarette, even though it's a non-smoking room. I don't bother reminding her. She's bought me a pepperoni pizza, and in between polishing off one slice and picking up another, I ask if Aunt Caro is going to help us out.

"Of course not." Smoke puffs out of her nose and mouth as she waves my question away.

Aunt Caro was one of the people we could've paid back with the money Ma's ex took to buy the truck. My mother squishes her cigarette into the base of the brass lamp on the nightstand, then pulls a small flask from her purse and takes a long drink.

"You know what's worse? Grandma's dead."

Already working on my third slice, I almost choke on a mouthful of hot cheese and pepperoni. Ma tilts her head back and takes another swig.

"The funeral was this afternoon," she says and wipes her mouth with her shirtsleeve. "And nobody bothered to tell me. My own *mother*, and they didn't even tell me. Can you believe that?"

"Well," I say, flicking a greasy mushroom off my slice. "You hated Grandma." Then I make it worse by adding, "At least she hated you, too."

Ma doesn't talk to me again until I've polished off the rest of the pizza by myself. Finally, I push the box away and ask: "So, is there anything for us?"

Ma shakes her head.

"There's not much left, anyway. Her house got flooded out. You remember how close it was to the river? Basically floated away down the Severn, like a little boat. Until it just—sank." She drains the rest of the flask in one gulp and lets it drop to the floor. "Anyway, we'll make it through. We always do—just me and you."

Ma glances over at me when I don't reply. Then she sits up, looking wildly around the room. "Where's Johnny Blue?" she exclaims, finally noticing the empty cage.

I look past her, at our blurry reflections in the dark window. Beyond our smudged faces, the sign for Welcome Home Motel flickers off, on, off, on. Rain slaps hard against the glass.

"He got away."

"Oh, kiddo, I'm sorry. You loved that bird." She leans over to pat my shoulder, slurring her words. "But don't homing pigeons have some instinct where they always know how to come back? That's their thing, right?"

"Yeah, I guess."

I don't remind her that we don't have a home for him to return to. Eventually, Ma turns the TV on. The preacher's long gone, replaced by the local news. Nothing's mentioned about a woman, her daughter, and a stolen Dodge Ram 1500. Ma slumps back among the pillows. The reporter's wearing a yellow raincoat and standing knee-deep in brown water, naming the surrounding roads that have washed away. If we stay too long, we could get trapped. There might not be a way out. I open my mouth to say something to Ma, but she's already out cold.

Later, she holds me so tightly in her sleep that I can't breathe. I wriggle away without waking her, slipping from the bed and curling up on the floor instead.

➤

I waken suddenly, sometime in the middle of the night. At first I can't tell why, but when I stir there's a sloshing sound. I sit up with a gasp. Water's seeping into the room from under the door, already lapping at my feet.

"Ma!" I shake her awake. "Ma, hurry up, we've gotta get out."

"What is it? The police?"

She's groggy, still reeking of drink. I tell her to go get the truck ready as I start shoving stuff into Ma's suitcase and my backpack, splashing around the room in cold water up to my ankles. The power's gone out, so I have to grope my way around in the dim light of the clock radio.

When I wade around the back of the motel to the truck, Ma's standing there with the keys, just staring at the rising water all around us. I throw the bags in the back and grab the keys from her before she drops them. She slouches against the truck's door, rubbing her forehead and groaning.

"Ma, you can't drive like this."

I take her by the wrist and lead her through the water to the passenger's side, where I half hoist, half push her in, and fasten her seatbelt.

"You're fourteen," she says weakly. "You don't have a license."

"Neither do you."

I close the door and wade around to the driver's side and climb in, placing Johnny Blue's empty cage between us. I adjust the seat, push the ignition button, and the engine purrs into life.

Ma takes my hand. We squeeze each other's fingers. Then I let go, leaning forward and gripping the wheel with both hands. In the sweep of the high beams, I can't tell what's river and what's road. I press down on the gas and we surge forward into the flood, water spraying out from both sides of the truck like dirty grey wings.

Half-Wild

I

Sylvia just barely catches sight of the animal in her high beams as it detaches from the darkness at the edge of the dirt road and flings itself in front of her Jeep. Accidentally slamming on the gas, she surges forward before stomping on the brake and being thrown headfirst, then back. Something in her neck cracks.

She unbuckles her seat belt, taking a deep, shaking breath. The immensity of the boreal night presses in on all sides. This winding dirt road eventually reaches her mother's house, but the surrounding forest stretches north and west, encompassing cold little lakes, long and unnamed rivers, and countless muskeg swamps.

When she finally grips the handle and swings the door wide, the night comes alive in a rush of dry heat and cricket song. An acrid note of smoke hangs in the dry air from the wildfires up north that have been burning all summer long. Afraid of what she'll find on the road, Sylvia slowly moves to stand where she can see the sprawled animal illuminated in the headlights. At least there's no blood. She kneels within an arm's length of the carcass, noting the short legs, blunt snout, and dark brown fur with golden-brown stripes running along the flank. She gags at the sharp smell—musky and rank. But despite having grown up in these woods, Sylvia doesn't have a name for the animal before her.

Then one of its hind legs kicks.

She staggers back, slipping on the loose gravel and dropping her phone. As she scrambles away she almost knocks herself out when she bangs her head on the Jeep's open door. Once inside, she sits with her eyes shut and slumps forward, resting her forehead on her knuckles. It's all been enough for one day. Enough.

When she looks up again, the headlights reveal a few metres of empty road ahead. Just like that, it's as though the animal was never there. Sylvia stares, mouth dry, scanning the narrow perimeter of light. There's nothing but the wide, watchful darkness all around her.

II

The only thing keeping her mother's old bungalow from being overtaken by the creeping growth of the forest is the garden, half-wild with herbs and medicinal plants. As Sylvia pulls up and gets out of the Jeep the porch light flicks on automatically, as though her mother could be up waiting for her. Catching the scent of spearmint in the overgrown grass by the front steps, Sylvia presses the back of her hand to her mouth and chokes back a sob as she pushes the door open.

Inside, she fumbles for the light switch. Glassy little eyes stare back at her from around the living room. Taxidermy was her stepfather's obsession, and his specimens still lurk around the house. A moose head looms over the TV set, and there's a stuffed bear cub tucked into a dusty corner by the window. A string of coyote tails dangles from the curtain rod, and a row of fluid-preserved little animals in jars lines the windowsill—possums and unidentifiable fetuses of various shades of pink or grey.

She reaches for a pickled possum and tilts the jar like a snow globe, watching the paws and tail rearrange themselves in the formaldehyde. She can't remember when she was here last—months, almost a year—but everything's just the same. Her mother kept all of these specimens in place, even after Stan was reported missing. Even after he was found face down in a snowbank after a winter thaw, bear mauled. By then it was already too late for Ruth. To the end, she lived as though Stan could still come roaring up from the grave, full of fists and rage again. As though it was his single, pickled eye staring from a jar on the shelf, not that of a long-dead wolf.

Stripping down to her underwear, Sylvia settles into the narrow cot in her childhood bedroom—another thing Ruth hadn't changed, as though the past were permanently fixed in place. A mounted snowshoe hare crouches on the windowsill beside the bed, glowing white in the gloom. It must have only been a few months old, just a leveret, when it was trapped and stuffed. As a child, it had given her nightmares. Later on, she felt sorry for it.

Sylvia rolls away and faces the wall. It's the first night she's ever spent alone in the house. She falls asleep remembering her mother's hands kneading the earth, with dirt-rimmed fingernails, tending to the plants she loved.

III

Sylvia wakes with a start, heart thrashing as though she's been running for her life. There was a predator with powerful jaws, sharp claws, a thick hide. She can still smell it on her, sense it lurking just on the other side of waking. In the dream, she was barefoot and bleeding, as the animal she'd hit chased her through the woods. Then she whirled around and chased it right back, running blind through the trees as it eluded her among the jack pine and tamarack.

She opens her eyes, and for a moment she doesn't remember why she's back in her mother's house. Sitting up, she almost cries out at the stiffness in her neck. Rising to make the bed, she draws back at the sight of blood on the sheets. Is she wounded somehow, or is the animal's blood on her? No—she checks herself and finds stickiness between her legs, a smear on her inner thigh. Relief washes over her, followed by guilt—warm, and then cold. So the treatment didn't work, and she isn't pregnant. Which means breaking the news to Idris all over again, with her husband's disappointment rubbing up against her own ambivalence about the future. She often can't quite think that far ahead.

Blank marble eyes follow her down the hall to the bathroom, where she showers and finds a tampon. In the kitchen, she makes instant coffee with condensed milk as the day takes shape around the tasks before her—she should call Idris, then figure out the funeral and deal with the paperwork. She ransacks the living room, looking for her phone, then recalls it dropping from her hand the night before, on the road. Outside, the morning air is already hazy with smoke from distant fires, and the sky is tinged yellow. Still, leaving the cluttered house is a relief. Then the Jeep roars to life and she's back on the road, dust billowing behind her.

Sylvia passes a few family farms, an abandoned quarry, and a beaver pond as she drives toward the spot where she came to such a sudden stop the night before. She pulls over by an unpaved driveway, marked by a dilapidated wooden fence, gets out, and finds her phone where she dropped it on the side of the road. The screen's cracked, but the phone still works.

Lingering by the gravel shoulder, she examines the road for signs—blood, fur, a claw come loose, or a fang. There's a vague set of tracks leading into the bush; just the hint of a trail through the dust. She can picture her mother squatting low and hovering her fingertips over animal prints, eyes closed, trying to discern who had raided her garden—voles, skunks, or maybe a fox. Sylvia gives it a try, and when she opens her eyes again a familiar old man is watching her over the crooked fence.

The old man taps the brim of his hat. Still crouching, she nods back.

"Is that little Sylvie, now?" the old timer calls out, squinting.

"It is." She gets up and brushes at the dusty knees of her jeans. "Good to see you, Mr. Carven. Been keeping well?"

He nods, coming around the end post of the fence and glancing up the road both ways. Then he unclips a tape measure from his loose leather belt and extends it between two posts. As far as Sylvia can remember, the fence has been halfway falling apart for the past thirty years.

"Come home, then, have you?" He gives one of the loose posts a little shake.

Sylvia rubs at her sore neck. She hasn't told anyone about her mother—hasn't texted her friends, or reached out to distant relatives or anyone else. Instead, she kicks at a stone in the road and tells old Carven the news, the first to know besides Idris.

"Ruth's dead."

Her words hover in the hazy air between them. Carven clips the tape measure to his belt again, nodding slowly.

"Last night had a feeling about it, eh?" he says. "Couldn't hardly sleep. Kept hearing an animal out there, yowling in the dark. Like something lost or hurt, or I dunno, haunted."

Sylvia bites the insides of her cheeks and recalls the moths flickering in the headlights, the pungent smell of whatever creature lay before her. Carven lifts his cap to scratch at his scalp with the brim.

"Real sorry to hear it," he says. "She was a strong woman, Ruthie. Too bad, the way things got."

Sylvia thinks of her mother's small, tremulous voice, and wonders if the two of them are remembering the same woman. Carven had known Ruth all her life, since he was a young man taking over his father's farm and Ruth was a little girl running around, climbing trees, singing to the cows, and getting into trouble. And he knew Sylvia when she was just the same. She wonders what he knows of her stepfather, and of her mother's sorrows at the end. Would he blame Sylvia for having left?

"Well now," Carven says, beckoning vaguely. "Why don't you come and get yourself some eggs, then?"

She follows him down the winding driveway to the make-shift chicken coops lined up behind his red clapboard house. Murmuring softly to the hens, Carven gathers six fresh eggs in a carton for her to take home. Sylvia shields her eyes from the sun as she gazes beyond the coop toward Carven's cattle pasture, where all seven jersey cows are lying down and ruminating in the shade.

"There you go." He hands her the carton. "Ruthie always loved the eggs fresh."

Sylvia thanks him, then gestures at the cows. "Must be hard for them, with the smoke and all."

"The rain's coming," he said. "When they lay down like that— means rain's coming. Maybe not today, but it's finally coming."

Sylvia can remember her mother saying the same thing, years back, and herself scoffing at the old wives' tale. She clears her throat.

"You know, I saw something," she ventures, as they walk around to the front of the house. "Last night, driving in. Some kind of animal ran out right in front of me. I hit it—got out and checked, but I've never seen anything like it. And then it was gone."

"Gone," he repeats. "Only stunned it, then, eh?"

"Yeah. But it was strange—kind of like a small bear, or a muskrat, but bigger, with a tail—"

She trails off, clearing her throat again.

"All sorts of creatures living in these woods," he says, gazing at the cows. "The fire's got them moving around, you know, the animals—coming up north or fleeing down south. Or could be something else gone feral, like hogs."

Sylvia considers this and thinks she understands. The forest keeps its secrets, just like everybody else.

"You take care of yourself, now," he says, patting her arm with a leathery hand. "A loss like that—it's the sort of thing that'll take some time."

Back on the road, Sylvia scans the gravel one last time before climbing into the Jeep and heading into town.

IV

Two days later, Ruth is laid to rest alongside her folks under her maiden name. The pastor whittles the silence into a few thoughtful words. Only Sylvia, Idris, and old Carven are in attendance. The unmoving air is signed with smoke; it still hasn't rained.

One by one, they each toss a carnation into the pit. Sylvia sways slightly, and Idris puts an arm around her. She could've gathered some wildflowers instead, or brought some of her mother's herbs to scatter over the casket. Something for deep sleep, for dreaming. She should've thought of that.

The back of her throat burns—the smoky air, the tears she's holding back. She should've called her mother more often, should've checked in after she'd left. She should've tried to re-connect. Even when Stan died, the distance between them had seemed too vast, too full of thorns to approach. She'd always blamed Ruth for staying with him, despite everything, to the end.

Sylvia squeezes her eyes shut, thinking of her mother living with Stan's menagerie. There was one animal he lusted after to complete his collection—a creature he never saw in the flesh despite spending most of his life on the land, hunting and trapping, around here and sometimes farther north. *Carcajou*, he called it in French. *Wolverine*. A powerful scavenger so secretive even experts don't know how many exist in the wild. Sylvia can still see her mother, back in the days when she had the will to fight back, hurling a stuffed goose at him, a wild look in her eyes as she taunted him, saying she hoped he never in his life found one.

As directed by the pastor, Sylvia takes a handful of earth to sprinkle into the pit. The dirt is hot and dry in her fist from baking in the sun. Even now, as she releases the earth onto the polished cherrywood of her mother's casket, there's a strained sort of triumph in knowing that there was one wild thing her stepfather hadn't claimed as his own—one living creature that had eluded his groping hands right to the end.

V

Sylvia and Idris spend the night at Ruth's house, saving the long drive back to town for the following morning. Idris gawks at the taxidermied animals around the living room, staring up at the moose head and then kneeling to examine the stuffed bear cub. He mimics the cub's posture, poised defensively with one paw raised and fangs bared, as though preparing for a fight.

"This is incredible," he says. "Creepy as hell, but also kind of genius, in a way."

"I don't know why she kept them all."

Sylvia settles on the brown tweed couch. The cushions are lumpy. She's letting Idris have the bedroom to himself, on account of his sore back after helping with the casket. She props a pillow up behind her own aching neck. Idris runs his fingers through the bearskin draped over the back of the couch, then flinches when he realizes that the flattened head, slack-jawed and empty-eyed, is still attached to the hide.

"Maybe she felt protected somehow—or less alone. The room does seem more alive, with all of them around."

"Except they're dead, and it's just sad."

Idris shrugs, turning to examine the row of specimens in jars. In a certain light, some of the baby fetuses look strikingly humanoid. They exchange a glance. Sylvia looks away first.

"What are you going to do with all of this?" he asks.

She's planning to pack all the animals up and drive them over to the town dump, but Idris wonders aloud if that might be a bit of a waste.

"Why, you think somebody would actually pay for them?" Sylvia glances around the room. "Maybe the rarer specimens?"

"I was thinking more like donating them to a natural history museum. Or maybe one of those visitor centres at a provincial park, where they have habitat displays and all that."

"I don't know," she says after a pause. "Maybe. There's a lot to think about."

They've already discussed selling the house. She can sense him compiling budget projections in an imaginary spreadsheet between them. His confidence in being able to plan for a predictable future usually comforted her.

"We'll figure it out," he says, leaning over and giving her a kiss.

He switches off the overhead light as he leaves the room. Moments later he calls out to her from the bedroom, and Sylvia remembers the bloody sheets with dismay. After seeing Carven that afternoon, she had returned to town to deal with the funeral—entirely forgetting about remaking the bed. She also hadn't mentioned it to Idris yet.

"I'll take care of it." She pushes past him into the bedroom. "You sleep on the couch instead."

"When were you going to tell me?" He stands at the threshold as she strips the sheets from the bed.

"I don't know," she says, as she locates fresh bedding inside a drawer in a nearby dresser. "Later. It's been a lot, with Ruth and the hospital and everything. I didn't want—"

"You didn't want to deal with it."

"No, I didn't," she says, finally meeting his gaze. "Still don't. I just—don't."

She viciously plumps up one of the pillows. She's sore all over, as though the ache in her neck is seeping down through her entire body, settling heavily in the pit of her stomach.

"We're not getting any younger," he says, his voice soft.

"Idris," she says. "My mother just died."

"Yes." He puts his hands up, stepping back. "You're right. I'm sorry. Now's not the time."

Idris closes the door as he leaves, and this time Sylvia doesn't go after him with entreaties or excuses. The stuffed white leveret peers up at her from the windowsill. She switches off the lamp and sits on the edge of the bed, half hoping Idris will slip back into the room and reassure her that they'll figure this out, too, along with everything else.

Sylvia pushes the window open. To her surprise, a light rain is finally falling. She takes several deep, steadying breaths. The night is thrumming and clicking with late-summer crickets.

As she breathes in the smell of wet earth and her mother's herbs from the garden below, there's a sudden guttural sound from the woods just beyond the house. A growl, a snarl, a snap of jaws. She catches the gleam of animal eyes—first here, then there. There's a sense of prowling, of circling the dark. She thinks: *wolverine.* Her heart pounds, as though it's come to find her. She catches a musky smell; whether real or imagined, she can't quite tell. Then the rain starts coming down harder, rattling in the eavestroughs and drowning out all other sounds.

Sylvia takes the stuffed leveret from the windowsill and sits back down on the bed. She holds it in her lap, stroking its silky ears. It's slightly damp from the rain. More than anything, she wishes she had the power to give its life back. That's what she would do with all of the specimens that were stuffed and silenced over the years, if she could—she imagines throwing open all the windows and doors so they could run, hop, slink, swoop, and crawl past her into the night, returning to the woods where they belonged.

Brave Daughter

The woman is walking through falling snow along Trulls Road, alone. Her name is Marie. At her age, she knows winter just as well as she knows the rivulets of veins on the backs of her hands. So much time has passed, and no time at all. Marie is a little girl, a grown woman. She is old. She's making her way to Muddy River, where she means to let the water finally take her.

Trulls Road is forested on both sides, until the bush gradually thins out into open fields. Here, the snow lies waist deep or higher, tunnelled under by vole, fox, and hare, while the surface weaves together tracks of lynx, deer, coyote, and grouse. But as a gale rises and brings flurries down with it, the windswept fields take on the appearance of empty space. Of vacancy.

The only sound Marie is aware of, as she drags herself through the snow, is the wind. It whistles through the grizzled strands of her hair, both propelling her forward and warning her to go home. No vehicles pass. Trulls Road takes her across abandoned railroad tracks, and from there she veers from the route and heads for the woods. Struggling through a snowdrift, she reaches for the naked young trees—grabbing at a thin trunk for

119

balance, then reaching for another to pull herself forward, and another.

Locating the trail, Marie finally picks up her pace. She takes long and definite strides, her footfalls crunching on the hard-packed snow. If somebody were observing her progress through the woods—the keen-eyed fox, for example, skulking on a ridge above the path—he would notice that Marie is wearing, rather strangely, a heavy bearskin coat. The fox catches the scent as she passes below him—the smell of living human mixed with the faint but recognizable scent of a brown bear. Marie glances behind her. Seeing nobody, she pulls the fur closer around her body and presses on.

The bearskin is an heirloom among the women of her family, passed down from her grandmother to her mother, and then to Marie herself. It was an object of intense fascination when she was a child, hanging first at the back of her grandmother's closet and later folded in the cedar chest at the foot of her mother's bed. She can't recall either woman ever wearing the bearskin as a coat. Instead, her mother would bring it out on those rare winter nights when the feeling came over her to tell Marie a bedtime story. She'd light a candle, and with the bearskin over her shoulders, get a distant look in her eyes. Then she'd begin: *This is the story of the brave daughter, who saved her mother from the terrible beast.*

She always recounted a variation of the same story, in which the daughter crossed a raging river, weathered a mighty storm, and fought off howling shadows to rescue her mother from a terrifying force that had already half swallowed her into its seething belly. Marie would pull the covers up to her chin as she listened to the harrowing adventures of the brave daughter, delighted by her mother's re-enactments, even as she sensed something prowling around the corners of the room.

You're putting nonsense into her head, her grandmother would scold from the threshold, arms folded across her chest. But she'd always lingered, eyes glinting in the candlelight as she followed along to the happy ending, when spring finally came and the daughter saved her mother.

On other occasions, Marie's grandmother had her turn with the fur, gathering it into her arms and spreading it across the bed. As she brushed the thick plush to keep it glossy, she told Marie a different kind of story. She conjured up the bear itself, and the lands it had once inhabited. There used to be lots of bears in the region—her grandmother's father had hunted and trapped them back in the last century.

One bear is enough to feed a family for months, she explained to Marie. *But now—well, you don't see many bears around anymore.*

Did they die out because of hunting? Marie asked, reaching out to run her own fingers through the black fur. *No,* her grandmother had replied. *Not exactly—because of clearing the land, development, more people around—all of it.*

Now, as Marie finally emerges from the forest onto the rocky banks of Muddy River, she shrinks from the blowing snow but keeps on walking. Arms outstretched and eyes squeezed shut, she steps out onto the ice. She knows these waters well, having played along the banks and in the shallows as a child. Farther downstream, the river splits into countless tributaries and shallow channels, braided with sandbars and rocky banks, broken up by beaver ponds and muskeg swamps that comprise the surrounding watershed. But she knows that the water runs deep and narrow here, well over her head.

Marie wears the bearskin now to wrap the memory of her motherline around her, but also because it's the densest item of clothing she owns—along with her heavy boots. She hopes the fur will bear her swiftly down, wrapped in the stories told by her mother and grandmother. Like the bearskin coat, this impulse has an inheritance of its own.

It was winter. It's always winter in Marie's memory, as though the past is one long, snowbound season with only brief glimpses of green and growing in between. Her mother always called it *the beast*, only half-joking. *Winter is the time when the old beast rises from his lair, stalking and hunting me.* But on that particular day, she had bundled Marie up in her snowsuit to go tobogganing with the twins from the neighbouring farm. She had spent the entire afternoon with them, playing a new game that the twins had invented: they would dare one another to angle their toboggans in a particular way, so that if they managed to hang a hard left, they could sail down the slope and skim over the bank, gliding out onto the icy river and extending the ride.

They had been expressly forbidden to do this, for fear of breaking through and falling into the frigid water, which meant that each ride was doubly exhilarating, combining the thrill of danger and the delicious fear of getting into trouble.

Marie had been having so much fun that she hadn't noticed the passing time—the sun was already low, the colour of milk and runny egg yolk on the horizon, before she remembered her mother's instructions to be home before sunset. Marie trudged back through the windswept fields with dread, dragging the wooden toboggan behind her. She left it by the back door and stomped the snow from her boots. Inside, the house was dim, shuttered. She called for her mother as she pulled off her sodden coat, apologizing for being late. She flung her coat over the radiator.

Ma? She had called into the silence. *Ma?* The house felt empty, and suddenly Marie was afraid.

Still wearing her snow pants, she waddled from the front hall into the kitchen, where the clock ticked into the hushed stillness. The stove was cold. She moved down the narrow corridor toward the bedroom, pushing the door open and reaching for the light switch. *Mama?* Spilled pills, her mother's unmoving shape under the quilt.

Marie did the only thing she could think of—she phoned her grandmother, who lived just down the country road. *Mama's sick*, she wailed. *I'm scared. Please come.* Her grandmother gave her a stern command: *Stay right where you are, Marie. Don't you dare move.* Marie thought she was in trouble, so she'd frozen on the spot. When her grandmother arrived, she found Marie still standing in her dripping snow pants by the phone in the hallway, her cheeks tear-streaked and raw from windburn.

I'm sorry, Marie howled as her grandmother embraced her briefly before hurrying to the bedroom.

For years, Marie halfway blamed herself—for being late that day, for not being a good girl, for leaving her mother alone in the dark. As her mother recovered, Marie tried to be well behaved so that her mother wouldn't worry, wouldn't get sad, wouldn't fall into that deep, lonely hibernation again. Even long after she knew better, she kept her grades up, came home on time, and stayed close by. Especially in winter. She came to understand how it hollowed her mother out. She remembered her stone-eyed grandmother, who often stayed with them, saying, *We keep one another alive through the winter.*

And her mother had survived. That was the important thing—she had lived, and she'd carried on living until the very end. And through the years, her mother added details to the story. *The brave daughter*, she would say as she tucked Marie into bed, *saved her mother from the wild beast. The brave daughter dragged her mother back from the claws of the terrible animal that grew from the shadows and stalked the woman through the short, lonely days and long, troubled nights.*

Sometimes the beast was big and bulky as a bear, other times it was smaller but wily, like a little grey fox or a jackal. Or fierce and secretive, like a wolf. Sometimes it was owlish, hunting at night on silent wings. *There are many forest creatures*, her mother always said, *but there's only one beast in the end.* Over the years Marie started feeling its presence herself—the heavy tread, the hiss and snarl, the animal weight on her chest.

Her mother had thanked Marie, near the end of her life. They had only ever acknowledged the incident in a fairy-tale way, sheltered by the bearskin between them.

Thank you for giving me life, her mother had said.

She was eighty-eight years old at the time, and there were tears in her cloudy eyes. Marie had smoothed her mother's wispy hair, murmuring.

>

Muddy River rarely freezes all the way through anymore—the ice is no more than a few inches thick at most. Some old timers can still recall when the river could be used as a winter roadway once the ice set in, and initially horse-drawn sleighs and then vehicles used the smooth expanse as a swifter way to traverse the winter terrain. Now, the township has set up signs at intervals along the banks: Danger! Thin Ice. Just last month a man fell through and had to be rescued by the fire department. The local paper ran the story with the headline: "Lucky to be Alive!"

Marie takes a few shuffling steps forward. The squall that swept up the snow as she worked her way along the trail has died down just as swiftly as it arose, more bluster than bite. Snow sifts and scatters, leaving patches of exposed ice. Upstream, around the bend and a few miles away, is the town. There, the river is funneled into a tight canal—a human construction. Marie turns and heads downstream instead, where the current widens into Goose Lake. The banks are lined with scrubby underbrush, willows and birches, and ever-steeper outcroppings of rock.

The ice edging the shoreline crunches into fragments under her boots. As Marie leaves solid ground, the texture of the ice surface changes—shifting from dry and brittle to more pliant. She can hear the muffled roar of the current below. Between and beneath her boots is bottomless black, all the way down. The ice shifts slightly under her weight, and she freezes, arms outstretched for balance.

Marie stands transfixed, staring into the abyss below. It suddenly strikes her, the fact that her mother reached a similar deadly brink, despite having a daughter and a family that re-arranged itself to fill the gaps when the depression took over. Even still, her mother had never quite escaped—she'd only kept it caged, just barely contained.

Marie imagines a long and unending sequence of interwoven lives—all of the women still living in her own blood, going all the way back into the first stirrings of ancestral time. An unbroken succession of mothers that would, soon enough, come quietly to an end with Marie herself. Sometimes she can feel their eyes on her, their shadowy features flickering. The women are silent, with outstretched hands that are bent and callused from lives of hard work, of rough weather, of raising children, of survival. *It's not my fault,* she wants to say. *It just happened this way.* Marie watches in despair as they turn wordlessly away from her.

A crow calls from somewhere nearby, breaking her trance. The bearskin hangs heavy on her shoulders. Marie takes another step, and the ice holds. She fixes her gaze on a crooked birch tree on the far bank before taking another step, lurching forward. The ice creaks as it bears her weight. A sudden loud crack reson-ates underfoot, reverberating through the ice, and Marie braces herself for the plunge.

This is the story of the brave daughter.

She had expected to feel resigned. She'd even expected to feel afraid. But she hadn't expected the sense of rage rising in her chest. What the hell is she doing in the middle of the bloody river, and how is she going to get back to land? She cautiously widens her stance, spreading her feet farther apart as she looks wildly around her—she can't turn back, and can't bring herself to move forward. A scream catches at the back of her throat, coming out as little more than a strangled whimper: *Help.*

She catches a flash of movement near the base of the birch. A tapered snout, dark paws, and shaggy red-brown fur—a fox.

He sniffs around the tree, and lifts his silver-tipped tail to leave a spray of scent in the snow. The ice beneath her feet makes another ominous pop. The fox looks up sharply, and his pale amber eyes lock on hers.

Marie suddenly sees the scene as if from above: there's an old woman wearing an absurd bearskin coat, teetering on thin ice, staring into the eyes of a little red fox on the bank. Beneath the ice, the current runs deep and strong, ready to swallow the woman down. The fox observes the woman's predicament and hesitates on the bank, unsure if she poses a threat. Then he sits back on his haunches, as though he's keenly interested in whatever happens next.

Marie returns to herself with a sudden sucking sound as the surface buckles and she instinctively drops into a crouch. She can't get back to her feet for fear of breaking through, and she can't look down again. She squeezes her eyes shut and counts. *One, two.* She puts both hands on the watery ice before her. *Three, four.* She opens her eyes. The ice is slick. Even on her hands and knees, it takes all her strength to prevent her limbs from splaying out. *Five.* She looks up and seeks the gaze of the fox again. His golden irises gleam. *Six.* Only now does she attempt to crawl forward, eyes still fixed on his.

As she reaches the far side of the river, Marie finds her footing and shuffles forward, her outstretched fingers clawing at the peeling bark of the birch. She hoists herself onto the bank and presses her palms against the tree, then the full, trembling length of her body, embracing it like an anchor. Gasping and coughing, she rests her forehead on the smooth bark. Her own breath, misting before her, is a miracle.

Marie looks for the fox, but all she sees is smooth, untouched snow blanketing the forest floor. Not even a set of tracks leading away into the woods.

Her legs are unsteady beneath her. She can't go back the way she came, with the risk of crossing the ice again. Instead, she'll have to take the long way around, walking downstream toward the rail bridge, where she'll be able to make her way back onto Trulls Road. From there, she can get home before dusk. Marie squares her shoulders, and wraps the bearskin more tightly around herself, around her mother, and her grandmother. Then she turns her back on the river.

Blue Coyotes

I

Hannah and her daughters had been at the old A-frame cabin at the dead end of Crooked Lake Road for only one night when the girls started going on about blue coyotes. At first, Hannah didn't pay much attention to their make-believe. She was busy trying to get the place habitable enough so the three of them could live there until she figured out what to do next.

Long before sunrise on the previous day, Hannah had slipped a fat envelope containing two months' rent under her landlady's door, before packing cranky, six-year-old Zoe and her dozing little sister Quinn into the back of the Ford Thunderbird, along with a few belongings from their apartment. She wasn't running away, Hannah had reminded herself during the fifty-kilometre drive from Ballycroy along backroads that drew them ever deeper into the woods. After all, there was nothing to run from.

It was well over a decade since she'd been here last, and she'd lost her instincts for getting around the backcountry. She pulled over a few times to consult an outdated roadmap, since there wasn't any GPS, but Crooked Lake Road wasn't clearly labelled. Instead, she found her way by following the tiny arrow that indicated the location of the now-defunct Chester Chemical Plant. She drove slowly down the long, skinny dirt road that gradually tapered out into an overgrown driveway marked by a weather-beaten, hand-painted NO TRESPASSING sign.

When the bush got too thick and the Thunderbird couldn't go any further, Hannah parked the car, and they went the rest of the way on foot. She held Quinn's hand as Zoe dashed ahead of them, calling out that she could see the lake through the trees. As they reached a small clearing where the A-frame cabin stood waiting at the edge of the woods, the first sight of the place after all of these years stopped Hannah in her tracks. Despite the peeling red paint, the old place still looked much the same as she remembered it. Consisting of a screened-in front porch, an open-concept living space, and a loft accessible by a narrow ladder, the cabin was surrounded by the traces of her mother's vegetable garden. The sagging front steps led down to the small, weedy lake—really more of an oversized pond—where she had learned to swim as a child. The vista of rolling hills on the other side of the water was marred by the concrete structure, which cast a long, jagged reflection across the rippling surface.

"Mom, what's that?" Zoe asked.

"It's an old chemical plant," Hannah said, shielding her eyes with her hand as she peered across the water. "Built back when I was a teenager."

"It looks kind of scary."

"Don't worry," Hannah said. "It was abandoned years ago."

"Why?"

"You ask too many questions, little lady," Hannah said, ruffling her daughter's hair.

Hannah set the girls up with notebooks and pencil crayons on the screened porch, then went in to start cleaning the cabin from the inside out. On the drive up from Ballycroy, she'd told them they were going on an adventure—almost like camping, only better, because they would stay at the cabin their grandfather had built in the middle of the woods. This had gotten the girls so excited that Hannah had started half believing the adventure story herself.

By leaving town for good, Hannah had figured that she could slowly start rewriting the past for her daughters. *Your father was a hard worker*, she would tell them. *A bit on the serious side, but he could also tell a good joke. He liked having a good time.* Quinn was too young to remember the violence. Zoe's memories, her mother hoped, would gradually fade or blend into Hannah's gentler version of the past. She would remind Zoe of the time Dimitri took her to fly a kite in the park, or how the family would all pile into the Thunderbird and make day trips to Georgian Bay when the weather was nice. That had only happened once, but Hannah thought it couldn't hurt to suggest it had been a few times.

These details would add to the other story she'd already told them, in hushed tones, about the night he'd died. Hannah had knelt before her daughters as they'd sat on the edge of the bed and looked them right in eye as she said, *Your father's death was a tragic accident. It's no one's fault—these things happen sometimes.*

Out on the screened porch, her daughters were talking in their little-girl language, laughing, whispering, and trying to mimic the whistled notes of a nearby chickadee. Hannah swept out the loft, where she laid out the girls' sleeping bags before descending the ladder and taking a scrub brush to the woodstove. She could still furnish the place in her mind exactly as it had been when she was growing up—her father's blood-red leather armchair in the corner by the window; the bearskin draped over the loft's railing; her mother's cherished portrait of St. Rita, patron saint of bad marriages and loneliness, propped up on the kitchen shelf; and her father's old shotgun on display above the fireplace.

He used to fire it three times from the porch to signal to Hannah that it was time to come home for dinner. The shots would echo around the small lake, sounding almost like a counting game: *five, six, seven, eight.*

Only it hadn't been a game. Hannah's face felt hot as she remembered running as fast as she could to reach the cabin before the last echo faded—and his fury if she took too long to get back. She shook her head, and the room was empty again.

After she dumped the stove ashes in a corner of the overgrown garden, Hannah went over to the porch to check on the girls. They were quiet as they concentrated on their drawings. Quinn's tongue was sticking out, and she was drooling slightly. Hannah bent to wipe the little girl's bottom lip with the hem of her shirt.

"Whatcha got there?" she asked, turning to her eldest. Zoe was holding up her drawing for her mother's appraisal.

"A coyote," Zoe said.

Hannah nodded approvingly at the bright blue canine on the page. "That's great, honey." She tilted her head to one side. "But shouldn't it be more grey?"

Zoe shook her head. "Nope, he's blue."

Hannah glanced at Quinn's drawing, and found that the toddler had scribbled a similar dog-like figure in a rich shade of aquamarine. Her daughters had always been crazy about drawing, but until now they hadn't shown any particular interest in depicting unicorns or fairies or magical beasts. Zoe usually focused on making her pictures as realistic as she could, becoming frustrated with her attempts at accurately portraying trees, animals, and little woodland scenes. Quinn, holding her pencil crayon in her fist, tried to follow her older sister's lead. Hannah was relieved to see that they were experimenting with colours, using their imaginations. She figured that a little fantasy was a good thing at their age, especially in the aftermath of their father's death.

Hannah left the girls to their artistic endeavours, taking a mop and bucket to the kitchenette. The clear water she'd filled the bucket with quickly turned grey as she scrubbed away the grime to reveal the faint cornflower blue of the cracked linoleum floor.

II

A week after the funeral, Hannah had taken a few items of value over to John's Pawn Shop in downtown Ballycroy, across the street from the hardware store where she worked part-time. The good-as-new toaster oven, and a gilded icon of the Virgin Mary that had belonged to her husband's long-gone mother, had produced enough cash that she'd been able to cover the overdue electricity bill—with just enough left over to buy new shoes for Zoe and diapers for Quinn.

The following week, she'd taken in her wedding ring for an appraisal, along with Dimitri's wedding band. It was a relief, getting that part over with. John gave her a sympathetic nod before squinting at the rings, holding each one up to the exposed light bulb swinging above the counter. Half the town had attended Dimitri's funeral, mostly workers from the local pulp-and-paper mill where he had been a foreman for years. There hadn't been any tears or signs of grief among the crowd. During the service Hannah had observed the grim faces all around her and got the feeling that she wasn't the only one still half-fearful of Dimitri's temper, even now that he was gone. There was no way around it. He'd been a hard man to live with and a hard man to work for, and in the end, as they said, it was his hard drinking that did him in.

John had given her a good price for the rings, maybe even a little more than they were worth, and offered her the full amount outright. He didn't comment on the nick in the band, which was from the night Dimitri drove his fist through the bedroom wall.

As John opened the cash register and thumbed through a stack of fifty-dollar bills, he told her in his slow, tight-lipped way, to hang in there.

"You're still young," he'd said, clearing his throat. "There's time enough yet."

Hannah had thanked him, keeping her eyes downcast as she did a few calculations in her head. She couldn't get more than a few shifts a week at the hardware store, and even with the extra cash from the rings she knew that by the following month she'd be struggling to make rent again. She dreaded the thought of having to find another place to live. Rentals were limited in Ballycroy, unless they moved into one of the beat-up trailers in the trailer park at the edge of town.

"How's your mother?" John asked then, pausing to lick his thumb before continuing to count out the bills. "I didn't see her at the funeral."

"Oh, you know. She comes and she goes."

John nodded. "But you've told her about Dimitri, I imagine."

"I've tried a few times, yeah. But you know how it is."

John frowned sympathetically as he slipped both rings into a drawer behind the counter. Hannah's mother lived in the old folks' home run by St. Rita's Catholic Parish. Most of the time she couldn't remember her daughter's name, or that she had a couple of granddaughters—even when they waved at her through the fence from the Catholic primary school across the street.

Hannah tucked the wad of bills into her purse and thanked John. When she turned off Main Street, she pulled out the cash as she reached her front steps, pausing to flip through the bills and double-check that there was more than enough to cover the rent for this month, at least. She also wanted to pick up a couple of notebooks and new coloured pencils for the girls, since they'd already worn their current set of Crayolas down to stubs.

"Well, would you look at that," came a voice above her on the stairs.

Hannah found herself under the gimlet eye of Muriel Burns, the sour-faced landlady who owned the two-storey duplex where she and Dimitri had lived since they first married. Muriel lived alone in the upstairs unit, and most of their encounters over the past few years involved Hannah apologizing for late rent, for bouncing cheques, and for the noisy disputes she and Dimitri had often had when he came home drunk.

But Muriel had started causing her a different kind of grief in the weeks since Dimitri's funeral. In fact, Hannah had figured that she could've stayed in Ballycroy after all—could've kept on living her life with the girls and no more than a prickle of re-morse about her husband's death—if it weren't for Muriel Burns constantly dropping by unannounced, asking about money and prodding her about the night Dimitri died.

"I hope you're planning to save some of that for this month's payment." Lips pursed, Muriel was eyeing the cash in Hannah's fist.

Hannah stuffed the money deep into her handbag. "Yeah."

"I hate to be a stickler," Muriel said. "But you do know you're two months behind?"

"I'm aware of the situation, Muriel," Hannah said, though she hadn't quite known the extent of it, and wondered bitterly how long she'd be paying off Dimitri's debts. "I'll have you know that I had to pawn Dimitri's wedding band for this—and my own ring, too."

"Oh really? So soon?" Muriel clicked her tongue.

"Look, I've got two growing girls in need of new shoes and three square meals a day, Muriel. But I'm sure you wouldn't understand." Hannah knew she should keep her mouth shut, but she couldn't help herself. "All I'm saying is, nobody's giving me a free ride."

"Well," Muriel said, with a knowing look. "I'm sure the life insurance will be a nice little bonus, eh?"

"Life insurance?"

With a flourish, Muriel handed over a blue envelope from the stack of local flyers and fast-food coupons in her hand. The envelope was stamped with the logo of a well-known insurance company. It had always irked Hannah that their mail was delivered to the same box.

"You know, I do pity your daughters," Muriel was saying as she thumbed through the flyers. "Growing up without a daddy. Girls should have a father."

Depends what kind of father.

The words were on the tip of her tongue, but Hannah swallowed them back.

"Anyway, take this, then," Muriel held out a flyer for the local grocery store, pointing out the discount coupons on the last page.

Hannah hesitated, then accepted the flyer with a nod. Still, there was something she didn't like about the look in Muriel's eyes—as though the woman was testing her, assessing Hannah's reactions.

She slipped into the apartment, where she dry heaved over the toilet before slumping into a chair at the kitchen table. Behind her, the tap dripped out an unsteady rhythm. Hannah slit open the blue envelope with a fingertip, which contained a letter from the insurance company informing her that further documentation was required to finalize the assessment. The mill must have submitted notice of his death. Suddenly she felt Muriel's eye on her again—watching through the window, waiting by the door, asking too many questions.

Hannah tucked the blue envelope and cash from the pawned rings away for safekeeping. Then she reached for the half-full bottle of Dimitri's vodka on the counter and raised it to her lips. Her throat burning, and suddenly the room felt stifling—as though all the air had been sucked out, the walls pressing in. Holding the bottle with both hands, she poured the remaining vodka down the drain.

She leaned unsteadily against the counter and glanced up at the clock. There was still half an hour before she was due to pick up the girls from school. She had just enough time to visit her mother at St. Rita's.

III

The simple red brick church and its outbuildings—the old folks' home, primary school, and community centre—served as a modest homage to the medieval saint after whom the parish was named. Hannah signed in at the front desk under a morose portrait of St. Rita, who watched over widows of murdered husbands as well as bad marriages and battered wives. It wasn't the first time she'd considered the trajectory from battered wife to redeemed widow implied by the saint's life story.

"Hi, Ma." The old woman had looked up at her briefly before her gaze drifted away to the window. "*Ma*," she repeated, kneeling before her wheelchair. "It's me, Hannah. Your daughter."

"Have you—accepted Jesus Christ—as your Lord and Saviour?" the old woman asked in her feeble voice.

"Sure, Ma," Hannah said. "The Lord is my shepherd, I shall not want—how's that?"

Her mother nodded, frowning slightly as she rearranged the grey folds of her shawl.

"Anyway, I just came by to tell you that Dimitri's gone. He's dead."

Her mother looked at her blankly, and Hannah wondered why she was bothering with this all over again. In a way, it was a relief knowing that in her mother's fading mind, Dimitri had never existed at all.

"It's just me and the girls, now," she added. "But you know, I think we'll manage."

"It's cold in here," her mother said.

Hannah reached out to help tuck the wool around her mother's legs, but the old woman drew back as though her daughter's hands were those of a stranger. Hannah sighed as she stood.

"The girls say hi. Zoe's starting first grade in September, and I can hardly believe it. Quinn's just three—she's in preschool. She doesn't talk much yet, but you should see how good she is at drawing—birds, cats, dogs, you know. I'll get her to bring you a picture the next time we visit."

"*Zoe*," her mother said, thoughtfully. "*Quinn*. Those are lovely names."

"Yes. They're your granddaughters' names."

"My granddaughters?"

"Don't worry about it, Ma. You don't remember. I'll be back in a week, and I'll bring the girls, okay?"

The old woman had given her a stony look. "I *do* remember," she said. "I remember the old house."

"The house?"

"Yes, the house—*our* house," her mother insisted. "At the very end of Crooked Lake Road. I can still picture it perfectly. Every window with a view of the water or the woods. My little garden, and the woods for you to run wild in as a girl. Remember listening to the coyotes singing all night, under the stars?"

Hannah returned her mother's fixed gaze, readying a retort about how it really was living in the middle of nowhere with a man like her father. And then he'd gambled off half the land, and the corporation had built the chemical plant, poisoned the lake to hell, and forced them out. But she faltered, and decided to give her mother this one.

"Sure, Ma," she said.

Her mother was looking out the window again.

"I bet it's still standing, that cabin, even after all these years. He was a good builder. Built the place to last, even when nothing else did."

The plan was already taking shape in Hannah's mind as she headed across the street to pick up the girls. If her mother was right and the old place was still standing, then it offered her an alternative—a place to both rewrite the past for her daughters, and get a fresh start herself. The cabin was close enough to town that she could still keep taking shifts at the hardware store and drive the girls to school. She would be able to live with a sense of independence, she considered, on her own family's land—at least until the insurance claim went through. She didn't want the girls growing up under Muriel Burns' roof, that's for sure.

IV

There'd been a freak snowstorm on the night Dimitri had died—April's final howler, the last laugh of winter before the sudden warmth of early spring.

He'd come home drunk again, blood on his knuckles from another bar fight. He'd stumbled in, angry and incoherent, making a racket that set Quinn wailing. The toddler had an ear infection and Hannah had only just managed to soothe her into a restless sleep. Hannah had shouted at him over the crying, and he'd pushed her against the wall—and then onto the bed.

Hannah struggled until she managed to wrench herself out from under him, nearly tripping as she fled to the threshold. He stood unsteadily, mumbling obscenities. She told him to get out and not come back until he was sober enough to apologize.

"Hannah—" he began.

"Not to *me*," Hannah hissed, gesturing toward the bedroom their daughters shared. "Apologize to *them*."

He'd finally backed off after that, lurching out the front door and letting in a blast of arctic air as he left. Hannah went back to console Quinn. The ceiling creaked above—Muriel Burns was awake, of course, and no doubt listening to the whole thing through the floorboards. Exhausted, Hannah drooped over the crib.

"Mama?" Zoe was sitting up in bed. "Why are you crying?"

"Not crying, sweetie. Mama's just tired, that's all. Go back to sleep."

When the toddler had finally quieted down, Hannah opened the front door and peered out into the storm. There was an unmoving shape on the walkway just beyond the porch. She pulled on her coat and stepped out into the cold. It wasn't the first time she'd had to drag her husband back into the house after he'd passed out. But this time, Hannah paused at the top of the stairs. Her shadow, cast by the light from the open door behind her, fell across his crumpled form, which was already dusted with snow. Hannah folded her arms across her chest. Stepping back inside, she nearly stumbled over Zoe, who was on the threshold behind her.

"Get away from the door," Hannah said. "It's snowing. You'll catch your death."

"Quinn's crying again," Zoe said, looking small in her thin pink nightie.

"Can you be a good big sister and help me give Quinn her medicine?"

Zoe looked past Hannah into the darkness, her mouth open to the blowing snow as though tasting the air. Hannah bent over her daughter to shield her from the wind, and from the sight of her father sprawled on the walkway.

"Come, Zoe," she said.

The little girl took her mother's hand, and Hannah shut the door behind them. She hesitated only slightly before she bolted the lock with a satisfying *thunk*. After administering Quinn's medicine and finally getting both girls to settle down for the night, she lay in bed staring into the dark. Above, the creaking of Muriel's footsteps had fallen silent. The house was quiet except for the wind rattling the windows, keeping Hannah at the edge of sleep for the rest of the night.

She rose at dawn, poured two glasses of orange juice, got out the girls' cereal, and prepared a pot of coffee.

As Zoe and Quinn ate their corn flakes, Hannah glanced out the window above the kitchen sink. A red sun was rising, and the snow on the walkway had crusted into ice overnight. Hannah stepped from the room and made a brief phone call, keeping her voice steady as she spoke.

When the paramedics arrived half an hour later, they pronounced Dimitri dead on the spot. Muriel Burns, who had emerged from her apartment and partway descended the snowbound stairs, let out a shriek at the news. Hannah wasn't wearing a coat, but even as she stood at the threshold she hardly felt the biting wind at all.

V

After spending the afternoon cleaning out the cabin loft, Hannah served up a dinner she had pulled together using the single-burner Coleman stove—macaroni and cheese with sliced hotdogs tossed into the mix. The three of them sat cross-legged on the screened porch, surrounded by a half-dozen of the girls' drawings. All of the pictures were of coyotes, and each coyote was depicted in a different shade of blue.

"All right," Hannah said, setting down her plastic fork. "So tell me about these coyotes."

Zoe straightened her back and cleared her throat importantly. Between mouthfuls, she told her mother how they had glimpsed the first coyote on the other side of the narrow lake, in front of the abandoned chemical plant. The coyote wasn't doing anything in particular, she said, but just sitting there, watching them. The next time, there were two.

"One big and the other little," Zoe explained. "They came closer, then ran away."

Hannah recalled hearing about a coyote who had carried off a local toddler by the scruff of his winter jacket.

"I want you to be careful, now," she warned. "Don't try to feed or follow any wild animals around here, okay? Coyotes are dangerous."

"I know," Zoe said. "But anyway, these coyotes aren't mean. Just curious."

"What do you think they're curious about?"

"About us. Maybe because they haven't seen us before."

"What about—unicorns?" Hannah asked, wanting to encourage Zoe's imaginative streak. "Do you think they might live around here, too?"

Zoe shot her mother a disdainful look. "No," she said. "Unicorns aren't real."

"Okay," Hannah replied, gathering up the Styrofoam bowls. "So where do you think the blue coyotes come from, then?"

"From the forest," Zoe said. Quinn gurgled something, and Zoe added: "Quinn thinks they come from the lake. She says maybe they were born underwater, so that's why they came out blue."

"How interesting," Hannah smiled.

"Mama, can we go swimming in the lake?"

"No, sweetie. It's still too cold."

"Soon?"

"That's not a good idea. Maybe we can visit a different lake when it gets warmer."

"But you said *you* used to go swimming here."

"Yes, but that was a long time ago. Before the factory spilled chemicals into the water."

Zoe looked at her quizzically, and Hannah set down her fork. "The water's toxic, honey. I remember when it happened—the whole lake died. All these fish started washing up on the shore, belly up, gills all black. The birds ate the fish, and then they died too, falling right out of the sky like stones."

Zoe stared, and Hannah held back on telling her about the family dog's tongue turning blue, and the litter of kittens born with strange defects.

"No playing near the water," she repeated. "I mean it."

After dinner, Hannah rinsed out the bowls with bottled water so she could reuse them for instant oatmeal the next morning. She wished she'd kept her mouth shut about the chemical plant. She could've persisted with the usual excuses—*the water's too cold, it's too muddy, you haven't taken enough swimming lessons yet.* Or simply: *sure, sweetie, let's talk about it when the weather gets warmer.*

She glanced out the window at the water. How long did it take for an ecosystem to clean itself out and become whole again? She remembered how the lake had turned a lurid shade of blue-green and gradually drained away down the river, poisoning the entire watershed. Maybe the three of them could work on regenerating the little lake together. That would be a good lesson for the girls to learn from their mother, she thought. On their next visit to town, she'd look up some plants that could help filter aquatic ecosystems naturally. But she also figured that, if left alone to the resilience of its natural cycles, the watershed would eventually be purified of its own accord. She was pretty sure that's how nature worked, anyway. An ecosystem would absorb the shock of contamination, and then figure out how to adapt itself.

VI

Later that evening, after putting Quinn to bed, Hannah and Zoe arranged the girls' drawings on the cabin wall. Their artwork, affixed with duct tape, helped cover up the peeling wallpaper and water stains that Hannah had already added to her mental list of minor repairs to deal with later. Zoe was still talking about the blue coyotes, describing how she and Quinn had spotted them playing in the shallow water, making strange noises in their throats that sounded almost like laughter.

"They live in the old factory," she said. "We saw one of them go through a broken window."

When they were done putting up the drawings, Hannah and Zoe stood on the porch together and watched the sun setting across the lake. Hannah imagined her daughters running around the property, growing up half-wild in the woods, burying Hannah's mixed memories of the place and exchanging them for better ones of their own. Her job, she told herself, would be to keep retelling the story of their survival, to filter the past so that it couldn't taint the future.

"Mama, do we live here now?" Zoe was looking up at her.

Hannah hesitated. "Yes, we're going to try to live here for a while. Just to see if we like it."

"Why?"

Hannah hesitated. "Sometimes, when you want to start over again, you have to leave other places behind. Even people, sometimes."

"Like daddy," Zoe said.

Hannah met her daughter's gaze. She opened her mouth to respond, then closed it again.

"Anyway, it's better here. It's pretty," Zoe said, looking out over the lake. "And quiet, too. Just us."

Hannah recalled what her mother had said: *a good place to grow up.* She released the breath she didn't realize she'd sucked into her belly.

"Just us," Zoe repeated. "And the blue coyotes."

After sending Zoe inside with a bottle of water to brush her teeth, Hannah lingered on the porch to watch the sun settle behind the imposing bulk of the abandoned chemical plant. A pair of loons were calling across the lake. All the make-believe stories she'd been telling her daughters had gone dry in her throat.

Then she caught sight of a flash of movement by the water. Something four legged was trotting along the shoreline. The animal paused to paw at something among the rocks. It was a skinny coyote. She watched as it was joined by a second, smaller figure, and the two coyotes made their way along a fringe of black spruce beyond the factory. They raised their heads and let out three high-pitched cries.

Hannah stood breathless. She would never have believed it. One coyote's fur was a vivid, almost electric blue, and the other coyote was a faded, chemical blue-green. They were otherworldly, and yet they entirely belonged there—they were unmistakably of the small, damaged lake and its surrounding woods, and even of the abandoned chemical plant. Somehow, this was their story.

Wild Girls

There's a solemnity in the way the two sisters trudge along the trail toward the river—in single file, with the older sister taking up the lead. Their mother has just died, and they aren't supposed to be out here alone. They're supposed to be at home, studying their math lessons and keeping the fire going. Their father left them in charge of the cabin. He said he would be gone for the day, taking the family's horse and cutter to make arrangements for their mother's burial in town.

Their mother would have wanted to be buried right here at the edge of the forest, in the rich earth that she loved to work with her hands. The girls know this, and their father does too. But it isn't a thing that is done, and in any case, the earth's still frozen. It's already mid-April, but in the forest, it still looks like winter.

Their father left in the morning when it was still dark, and by the afternoon the sisters were already bored. They made savoury oats for lunch, and then brought in more logs from the shed and stacked them next to the woodstove. They did sums and read to each other from *The Red Fairy Book*. They pulled on their coats and boots and took turns using the outhouse. And then, they stood at the edge of the woods and listened to the trees creaking under the weight of ice and snow.

It was the little sister who noticed the fresh tracks leading down the trail their father had long ago hacked out from the surrounding bush. They both recognized the evenly spaced hoof-prints of a white-tailed deer, with drag marks loosely connecting each print. Glancing at each other, they started heading down the path—letting the snow's memory of the deer guide them into the bush.

Now, it's as though the forest senses their presence as soon as they step onto the trail. There's a braced stillness, a watchfulness. The chickadees fall silent. Dead leaves rustle. The trees have eyes. The girls pause before a stain of blood on the snow, framed by a spray of wing markings. A hawk, or maybe an owl, swooped down and struck its prey only moments before they arrived.

The sisters step over a massive oak that has fallen across the trail, and the older girl says they must tell their father about it—he'll have to clear it out when the snow melts, which should be any time now. There's the smell of a thaw in the air, and it's finally milder than it's been in months. The girls identify the tracks of red squirrels, rabbits, and something between canine and feline that the younger sister determines must be a fox. They note the markings of a grouse that had burrowed down and suddenly took flight, leaving traces of wing prints fanning across the snow.

The sisters pause to assess each new pattern of tracks. They examine scat, dropped feathers, little burrowed places, and tufts of fur, putting together the interweaving stories as their mother taught them to do. Sometimes the sisters think they know the bush better than they know most people. Almost as well as they know each other.

Eventually the trail splits in two, and without exchanging a word the girls choose the path that leads down to the river. Along the way, the deer tracks are joined with those of a very different mammal. Large, deliberate, and canine—easy to identify as a wolf's. The sisters draw closer together, but they don't turn back. Instead, they follow the wolf's tracks, like the wolf, in turn, had shadowed the deer.

At the place where the river meets the lake, criss-crossing prints veer off into an area where it's not clear what's land and what's ice. They don't dare follow. The younger sister sinks down onto a nearby stump, complaining that her legs are tired from struggling through the snow. The older sister blows into her cupped hands for warmth.

Neither sister mentions what they've really been looking for as they wander through the bush. They hoped to find their mother's tracks in the snow. She'd brought them here just the previous week, leading the way and showing them various animal markings along the very same trail. They'd spent the rest of the afternoon setting up spouts and buckets for maple tapping. But it's snowed since then—one of those wet, late winter snows— burying the memory of that day and concealing any lingering trace of their mother's living presence in the bush.

The sisters listen for the sound of running water below the thinning ice. The older girl pulls a couple of snacks from her coat pocket—somehow, she ended up bringing along little bundles of nuts, which her sister prefers, but neglected to bring dried fruit for herself. Sometimes they forget that they don't always like the same things.

The younger girl puts a handful of snow into her mouth, let- ting it melt on her tongue and wash the nuts down. Her sister lifts the lid of a nearby maple-tapping bucket and peers in, sur- prised to find it nearly full of transparent sap already. She dips her finger in and samples the sweetness. Then she helps hoist her little sister up so that she too can have a taste, but she loses her balance in the loose-packed snow and they both fall face-first into the icy white. Sitting up, the older girl points to a distinct animal print in the undisturbed snow nearby. They both crawl on hands and knees to get a closer look, exclaiming in a single voice, "Bear!"

The sisters take turns pressing their palms into the deep impression of the track, which is double the length and width of their small hands. Wordlessly, they start following the tracks—not in the direction the bear was heading, but backtracking to where it had come from. On the other side of the clearing, they come across a deep hollow at the base of a maple tree. Peering into the dark space, the sisters sense warmth from within. There's a shuffling sound, and it takes them a moment to realize that a little bear is staring straight at them through the gloom. The sisters keep still, holding their breath.

They know they're supposed to make a lot of noise, supposed to wave their arms, and make a loud scene. Their mother had warned them countless times about bears, and they've always been good girls. But through a shared childhood spent playing hide-and-seek among the trees, these sisters have gotten to know the way of the woods around them. They've learned when to run, and when to hide. They've learned when they shouldn't speak, and how to converse with each other using only the slightest gestures. From their mother, who also grew up on the land, they've learned how to blend into their surroundings, keeping their breath slow and even until danger passes. They've learned when to call for help, when to hold their ground, and when to run back home. And they've learned how there's a way of carrying on in the woods, not as though they're prey or predator, but as though they belong there—part of the wild intimacy of all things living, dying, and decaying among the tangled roots and branches.

As the cub blinks up at them, the sisters both realize that the mother bear is not in the den with the youngster. They glance at one another with a shared flicker of fear. It's early spring, just about the time when bears rouse themselves from their slumbers, shake the winter-long stiffness from their bones, and come rumbling up to satisfy their hunger and thirst.

As the cub snuffles at them, uncertain of his own curiosity, the girls start backing away. In a coordinated series of movements, they crab crawl several paces through the snow, then stand, turn, and bolt, hand in hand, toward the river—suddenly fearful of the hushed surroundings of the bush, seeking instead the open expanse of river mouth and frozen lake beyond.

At the riverbank they lose their footing, and their grip on one another's hands. The older sister lands on her hands and knees, snow biting into her wrists where her coat sleeves have been wrenched back. She stands, wincing, just as the ice breaks open with a terrible crack. She watches in dismay as the river swallows her little sister right up.

>

The cub was born in the depths of winter. For months, the den has been an extension of his mother's womb; he's spent the winter moons drinking her rich supply of milk, nuzzling blindly at first, his fur growing thicker, dreaming the feral dreams that the forest breathes into him. He hasn't yet learned to be wary, to quite feel afraid. After his mother leaves on one of her excursions to find food and water, the strangers arrive at the den. When they disappear as quickly as they came, he grows curious. He makes his way through the snow and rises onto his hind legs, crying out for his mother.

The cub is familiar with the constant roaring sound of the nearby river; its resonance has filled his dreams since birth. But the sudden scream is something new. He sees the two figures at the bank, and watches as one of them falls. But the cub focuses on the dark shape of his mother, to whom he is magnetically drawn. She's nearby, unnoticed by the fleeing visitors as she dashes a hole in the ice with a powerful paw. She slakes her long winter's thirst, splashing around as one of the figures disappears into the dark water upstream.

The cub calls out to his mother, and she drinks for a few moments longer before turning and ambling back toward him. She's still half in a stupor; it's early in the new season, and there's a little time left for dreaming. Together, they den back down.

On her knees at the riverbank, the older girl shrieks for her sister. She bangs her fists on the ice until blood appears. Then, abruptly, the little girl bursts up from the water, hands outstretched, scrabbling at the hole that the mother bear made for drinking. Gasping with the effort, her big sister hauls her from the water. Weak with sobbing, the sisters cling to one another. The younger one trembles—her hair frosting over, lips blue tinged. The older girl peels off her sister's coat and replaces it with her own, then bends low so the younger one can latch onto her back. She braces herself, adjusting to her little sister's weight. Then she runs, following their own tracks back home.

Acknowledgements

Many thanks to the Toronto Arts Council for their financial assistance during the final stages of completing this collection.

My warmest gratitude to Dianne Warren, whose mentorship was invaluable in shaping this manuscript from the beginning. Thanks to Liz Philips for the enthusiasm, clarity, and insightful editing, and for seeing this project to the end. It's been a pleasure working with the team at Thistledown.

My thanks to the Humber School for Writer's graduate certificate program in creative writing, which enabled me to develop this collection.

I'm grateful for the Writers' Trust and their work in recognizing emerging writers. Special thanks to the 2022 short fiction judges of the RBC Bronwen Wallace Award, Erin Frances Fisher, Angélique Lalonde, and Derek Mascarenhas, for their attentive reading of "Wild Girls."

"Bear Bones" was originally published in the *Humber Literary Review*, and an earlier version of "My Father's Apiary" was longlisted for the CBC Short Story Prize. Many thanks to Isabella Fink and Shirarose Wilensky for their editorial advice.

All my love and gratitude to: Mom, for nurturing our imaginations. Dad, for the bees, the cabin, and the walks in the woods. Mary, for showing us the secret spots along the way. Laura, for all the time shared outdoors. Andrejs and Giulia, for the forest itself. Lewis and Eleanor, for the unforgotten place across the lake.

Many thanks to the friends who have seen me through this: Kyra, for the pep talks and adventures. Bergita and Klaudia, for the meandering conversations. Gabi, for the shared understanding.

And always, all my love and thanks to Gerardo, for the daily patience and support.

EMILY PASKEVICS is a graduate of the Humber School for Writers. Her work has appeared in several publications, including *Vallum Magazine*, *The Humber Literary Review*, and *Hart House Review*. In 2022 she was a finalist for the Writers' Trust of Canada's RBC Bronwen Wallace Award, for her short story "Wild Girls." She was also longlisted for the 2019 CBC Short Story Prize for her story "Little Wild Creatures." She divides her time between Toronto and Montreal.